About the author

Linda Newbery taught English in various schools before becoming a full-time author, and a regular tutor of writing courses for children and adults.

She has written a number of books for young adults, and has been twice nominated for the Carnegie Medal, and also the Writers Guild Award.

Linda lives in Northamptonshire with her husband and three cats.

The *Moving On* trilogy by Linda Newbery

No Way Back
Break Time
Windfall

ORCHARD BOOKS
96 Leonard Street, London EC2A 4XD
Orchard Books Australia
Unit 31/56 O'Riordan Street, Alexandria NSW 2015
First published in Great Britain in 2001
A PAPERBACK ORIGINAL
Text © Linda Newbery 2001
The right of Linda Newbery to be identified as the
author of this work has been asserted by her
in accordance with the Copyright,
Designs and Patents Act, 1988.
A CIP catalogue record for this book is
available from the British Library.
1 84121 584 8
3 5 7 9 10 8 6 4 2
Printed in Great Britain

BREAK TIME

Linda Newbery

ORCHARD BOOKS

*For Penelope Dunn
– at last!*

Mountain Bike

The school bus passed Jo while she was puffing up the hill out of Farthingfield. The bus was two-thirds empty, as always by the time it got this far; the few remaining passengers were crammed into the seats nearest the back. A row of grinning faces looked out of the back window at Jo, and Jason Reed stabbed a finger at the side of his head and swivelled it. Jo took no notice. Coping with the sluggish temperament of Mum's old bike in its lowest gear was hard enough, not leaving a hand free to signal something rude back.

If the weather was foggy or freezing, Jo used the school bus too, but on an average winter day like today she preferred to cycle. Five miles to Hagley Heath and back each day kept her fit, and she liked the independence the bike gave her: better than standing about shivering when the bus was late, which it often was. Jason Reed thought she was mad, especially in view of the decrepit state of the bike.

'Hey, Joke! Want some Sellotape to hold it together?' he'd shouted today from the bus queue as Jo pedalled off. Joke was what the boys in her form called her, because her name was Jo Cannon – Joke Annon. Jason would have thought she was even more of a joke if he'd seen the brand-new, twenty-one speed mountain bike sitting in the garden shed at home. It was almost worth turning up at school on it just to see his face.

The mountain bike was one of two things worrying Jo as she reached the top of the rise, changed to a higher gear and sat down, easing the aching backs of her legs as the pedals started to turn more easily. The other problem was in her rucksack.

'Make sure you hand these over at home,' Mr Kershaw had said at afternoon registration when he handed out the letters. 'I want the signed bits back tomorrow. Even if you don't want to go. I'm not having anyone's parents complain they didn't see the letter.'

Lynette leaned forward to snatch one from the row in front. 'Great! Outdoor Activities Week at Penwhatsit! I'm definitely going, are you, Jo?'

'Mm, yes, I expect so,' Jo said. In fact, as Mr Kershaw was explaining, no one was *definitely* going to Penhowell: there were always more people wanting to go than there were places, so all the names went into a bag and only thirty were picked out.

But to have your name put in the bag in the first place you had to be able to pay £150. Jo's mum hadn't got £150, or at least not £150 that wasn't already destined for something more important. All her spare money had gone on carpets for the flat, and a washing machine, and getting her ailing car serviced. Jo didn't even want to ask, but the letter was there in her rucksack and Mr Kershaw would want the signed reply tomorrow – he was the teacher organising the trip, and expected everyone to be as enthusiastic as he was. Jo would have to pretend she wasn't interested in going. 'Mum, we've got this letter, something about a trip to Wales,' she could say, casually. 'I don't want to go, so just sign this to say so, could you?'

But then Mum would read it – Mum always read letters from school, really carefully, twice – and she'd know straightaway that Jo would love to go. It was just the sort of thing Jo loved to try. Mountain-walking. Pony-riding. Canoeing. Rock-climbing. In Wales, in the Black Mountains and the Brecon Beacons, for a whole week. Jo thought of herself sitting in Assembly and Maths and History for five whole days while her luckier friends set off each morning on ponies or in canoes. It wasn't fair! She hadn't complained about moving away from Hagley

Heath, not once. She hadn't complained about moving to the flat she and Mum shared with Nan, even though it meant living miles from her friends, and not being able to dash down the road to see Lynette. There would have been no point complaining, anyway. But this was a bit much – she wouldn't have minded if there hadn't *been* an outdoor pursuits trip, but the fact that there *was* one, and she wouldn't be going on it, seemed like punishment. Punishment for something that wasn't her fault.

Jo reached the new road that by-passed Beckley and cycled through the new housing-estate that was groping its way slowly outwards to fill up space at the edge of town. There were still more houses being built; the earth was all churned up and there were roof-timbers lying flat on the ground like bits of Meccano kit. House-kits. The finished houses looked a bit like children's toys too: they had beams and gables, Georgian pillars and porches, brickwork in fancy patterns, as if the designers hadn't been able to decide on any particular style so had chosen a bit of everything. A few were already occupied, with swagged curtains at the windows and shiny cars outside. Jo could bet that nobody in one of those new houses had an ancient bike like hers. People who lived in that sort of house would have everything shiny and new and up to date, even their Tudor beams and Victorian brickwork.

Jo preferred the old High Street, where there was still a market on Thursdays and an old town hall and little shops that sold clocks and farm equipment and flowers. Mum and Nan both worked in High Street shops, and both of them complained about the new Sainsbury's and DIY store out on the by-pass, that were taking business away from the town. 'It'll be a ghost town, soon,' Nan would say, looking out the gift-shop window. And Jo would imagine see-through ghosts walking about in twos or threes with shopping bags and trollies, comparing prices and showing each other what they'd bought.

Nan worked in a shop that sold completely useless items: tiny glass vases that were too narrow to put more than a single stalk in, delicate china animals that Jo was sure would tumble off the shelves and crash to the floor if she so much as looked at them, paintings of thatched cottages and milkmaids, and shiny headscarves covered with stirrups and snaffles. All of them were horribly expensive. Mum's shop, *Harvest*, was much nicer: full of spicy smells and home-made cakes and interesting things in little bags. But, when Jo parked her bike in the side alley and went in to collect the key, there was only one customer in the shop: a very old lady in a tweed coat and thick stockings, counting out her money to buy one vegetable pastie and a packet of dried apricots. Wrapping up the pastie, Mum looked up at Jo with a tired smile; the doorbell rang cheerfully as the old lady went out into the street. Poor old Mum. What she needed was people coming into the shop in gangs, demanding pasties by the dozen and apricots by the barrowload. All the building-site workers, perhaps, suddenly turned health-conscious. But they were far more likely to go down to the new Burger King next to Sainsbury's.

'Hello, love. Had a good day?' Mum said.

'Yes, thanks.' Jo knew straight away that she wasn't even going to mention the outdoor activities letter. It wouldn't be fair on Mum. She wondered how many cartons of soya milk, how many pasties and prunes Mum would have to sell to make anything like £150. A mountain of health food reared up in her imagination, so vast that she could walk up it and camp at the top. No. She wasn't going on the trip; she'd have to get used to the idea.

She went round the back to put her bike away in the shed. Inside, leaning against the wooden wall with an air of faint distaste, as if it thought it inappropriate to consort with unwashed flowerpots and seed-trays, was the mountain bike. Its handlebars turned up slightly, reminding Jo of those shaggy cattle with huge sticking-out horns. Its metalwork gleamed, with black and scarlet letters bragging its brand-name. Jo heaved the old bike inside and leaned it against the window side, not touching. She fancied the mountain bike would give a shiver of distaste if it came into contact with Mum's rusty old rattletrap. It hardly considered itself to be a member of the same species.

Mountain bikes cost more than £150. A lot more.

If Jo took it back to the shop, she could say there had been a mistake and she didn't want it, then pay for herself to go on the trip.

But no, of course she couldn't. Common sense stepped out from a corner of her brain to put her right before she got too carried away. Of course she couldn't. Dad had bought her the bike and he'd expect her to be using it on the weeks when she stayed with him. Next Monday, for a start.

Jo closed the shed door and went up the fire-escape to the back door of the flat, thinking about it. If she stuck obstinately to her old bike, it would hurt Dad's feelings, after he'd spent all that money to give her a wonderful surprise. If she rode the new bike to please Dad, it would feel like being disloyal to Mum. Why did life have to be so complicated?

Nan

Jo's mum and dad had explained it all to her, last summer. Once they'd decided to split up, they stopped behaving like moody teenagers, obviously deciding to be calm and adult, sorting out their savings and mortgage and building society accounts and only arguing in a polite and controlled fashion about who owned which books and records.

Jo had made up her mind to be adult about it too. The way things had been going – rows; silences, red-eyed misery (Mum), tight-lipped anger (Dad), and anxious exasperation (Jo) – it was obviously best for everyone if they stopped trying to live together, stopped trying to be a proper family. Jo could handle that. It wasn't unusual, was it? People's parents split up all the time. You only had to look round her form group. There was Nathan Fuller, for a start; everyone knew about Nathan. And Samantha Warburton, whose dad lived in Australia now. Amanda Flynn had a step-dad, and had acquired a gorgeous older stepbrother, Luke, as part of the package. (Ellie Byrne, Amanda's best friend, was secretly and devotedly in love with him. No one was supposed to know, but Amanda had told Jo in confidence.)

Jo was just another statistic. A member of a one-parent family.

Except that she hadn't got only one parent. She had two. That was the problem. And now that Nan was living with her and Mum, she might as well have three.

'Earl Grey for me, dear, if you've got the kettle on.' Nan, as usual, was in before Mum. 'My cup's on the drainer. And don't forget to warm the pot, will you, dear? I know Stephanie never bothers but it does make all the difference.'

To Nan, Mum was always Stephanie, never Steff which was what Mum called herself. Nan went into her bedroom to take off the smart navy court shoes that made her corns hurt, and Jo took Nan's bone china cup and saucer from the draining board and set them on the tray next to the stoneware mugs she and Mum used. The cup was so thin you could almost see through it, and the handle so fragile that Jo was certain it would snap off if she so much as touched it. Nan liked tea served properly, not just sloshed into mugs but served on a tray, with milk in a jug and sugar cubes in a bowl.

It was funny about Nan. Before, when she had lived twelve miles away, visits to or from Nan had been a weekend treat. Now that Nan was sharing the flat with Jo and Mum, well...

It wasn't that Nan didn't mean well. She did. That was why she'd put her money into the shop and flat, to help Mum get started. She was concerned about every aspect of Jo's and Mum's lives, as if her own wasn't enough for her and she wanted a share in theirs too. She would read Jo's homework over her shoulder and point out spelling mistakes (Nan prided herself on her spelling) and she would sniff round the kitchen while Mum was trying out a new recipe for the shop, turning over the packets of exotic spices with the tips of her fingers, as if Mum were trying to sneak illegal substances into the flat. If Jo's English teacher failed to correct a spelling mistake in her book, or if Mum's recipe for mince pies used vegetable fat instead of suet, Nan wanted to know why.

Nan liked things Nice. That hadn't mattered when she lived on her own. The Niceness of Nan's bungalow had been part of Jo's childhood – the glass ornaments on the mantelpiece, the iced sponge-cake for tea, the sweet peas Nan grew in the garden and brought indoors in vasefuls to spill their sugary scent on the air. Now Nan had her own room and she kept that Nice, but she would never be really happy until the entire flat was Nice too. As Jo and Mum were both incurably untidy, Nan looked like having a long campaign on her hands. But this didn't deter her at all.

'You can't blame her,' Mum always said, when Jo found Nan's tidying-up and helpful hints a bit too much. 'It's been quite an upheaval for her, after living on her own for so long. And without her, I'd never have been able to set up the shop.'

Waiting for the tea to brew, Jo heard Mum's slow, heavy tread coming upstairs. Mum always looked tired these days, as if she were lugging an invisible burden around with her. Nan, apart from wincing a bit when her feet hurt at the end of the day, looked far more sprightly, and often ran up the stairs like a ten-year-old. Nan had worked in a knitting shop until it closed down, and had been lucky to find just the right job when she moved to Beckley – a Nice job in the gift shop, *Thinking of You*. (Jo considered this to be an utterly stupid name for a shop. If you ever went in to buy something for yourself – not that she could ever imagine wasting her money on such expensive tat – you'd have to feel selfish for *Thinking of Me*.)

'Oh, is that tea?' Mum said, closing her eyes and walking towards the kitchen table on autopilot. 'Just what I could do with.' She sank into a chair and kicked off her shoes (what *was* it with adults, Jo thought, that made them incapable of choosing comfortable shoes?) as wearily as if she'd trekked for hours across desert wastes in search of an oasis. Jo poured the tea and took Nan's cup through to the main room, where Nan had turned on the TV. Neither Jo nor Mum specially liked the perfumey taste of Earl Grey, but it was easier to give in to Nan.

Jo's homework books were spread out on the table – a chart to complete for Geography, two chapters to read for English, and some French irregular verbs to learn – and so was The Letter, or rather what remained of it. Jo had already cut off the main part of the letter which explained what it was about, leaving only the reply slip. She had crossed out the bit which read *I would like my son/daughter's name to be entered for the draw*, leaving the words *I do not want my son/daughter to participate in the Outdoor Pursuits course*. Perhaps, she thought, she could get Mum to sign it now. In this semi-soporific state there was a chance she might sign her name without asking awkward questions.

'Oh, Mum,' Jo said as casually as she could. 'Just sign this, could you? It's nothing important.' She handed over a pen with the letter and pretended to carry on learning verbs, really watching closely from under her fringe.

Mum unscrewed the pen top and had almost started to write when she put down the pen and looked at Jo closely.

'Jo, what is this? Where's the letter that goes with it?'

'...*atteignons, atteignez, atteignent*,' Jo recited, nonchalantly. 'Oh – can't remember. Doesn't matter.'

'Outdoor Pursuits?' Mum pursued. 'Come on, where is it? Is it in your bag? If it's a letter to parents I want to see it before I sign. And you can't tell me you're not interested.'

'Not interested in what?' said Nan, entering the kitchen with her bone china cup and saucer held carefully in front of her.

'There's a letter about an Outdoor Pursuits course,' Mum explained, 'and for some reason Jo's pretending she doesn't want to go.'

'Well, perhaps she *doesn't* want to go.' Nan dropped an extra sugar cube into her tea and then stirred it, with the faintest of reproachful looks at Jo for not getting it right. Jo had forgotten that Nan liked it practically like syrup. 'What is it anyway – rock-climbing and that sort of thing? Sounds dangerous to me.'

'It wouldn't be dangerous,' Jo couldn't help explaining. 'Not with the instructors they have, and ropes and safety harnesses and all that. You have to learn how to do it safely. That's the whole point. And it's not just rock-climbing. They go pony-trekking and canoeing and—'

She stopped abruptly. She hadn't been able to help sounding keen, and now Mum was looking at her with a puzzled expression.

'Sounds good fun. But it's hardly part of the school curriculum, is it?' Nan said. 'It's not going to help you through your O-levels.'

'GCSEs, Nan. O-levels went out donkeys' years ago.'

'If you ask me, you'd do far better to spend a week in Paris visiting art galleries and improving your French. Your accent is *terrible*,' said Nan, who considered herself an expert on French culture since visiting the hypermarket near Boulogne on a day trip.

'But I won't even be doing art next year.'

'And I bet the school expects you to pay for this outdoor holiday,' Nan persisted. 'How much is it?'

Great. Thanks, Nan.

'Yes, how much?' Mum said. 'Where's that letter, Jo?'

Jo rummaged in her rucksack. 'I don't know why you're both so interested. I didn't say I wanted to go, and anyway there's only thirty places and about a hundred people who want them. If you just sign that slip, Mum, I can give it back to Mr Kershaw tomorrow.' She handed the crumpled piece of paper across the table to Mum, who smoothed it out and read it carefully.

'A hundred and fifty pounds,' Nan said, leaning across to read it too. 'Always expecting you to fork out, that school. If it's not one thing it's another. Minibus appeal, theatre visit, charity fundraising. They must think we're made of money.'

'You'd really like to go, wouldn't you?' Mum said, looking across the table at Jo.

'I told you, there's not much chance anyway, so there's no point thinking about it,' Jo said, wishing they could finish with the subject. There must be something else they could talk about: how samosa sales were today, or whether there had been a sudden demand for snaffle key-rings or glass hedgehog paperweights...

Nan darted a look at Mum. 'You could always ask Richard to pay up for this trip of Jo's, if she wants to go. He can afford it.'

Mum didn't answer. She clasped her mug with both hands as if she suddenly needed warming up.

'No!' Jo said. 'Not Dad. He's just bought me the mountain bike. I'm not asking him for anything else.'

'He shouldn't need asking,' Nan said. 'He always was a bit tight with money if you ask me.' She was talking to Mum rather than to Jo, but Mum was staring into her tea as if she found something interesting there. Not at all deterred, Nan turned to Jo and said brightly, 'You could ask him next week. When you're staying over there.'

'Nan, I've *told* you! I don't specially want to go, and I'm *not* asking Dad to fork out!'

'Well, I don't see why he shouldn't pay. I'll ask him myself, if you're afraid to.'

'I'm not *afraid*—' Jo looked at Mum, hoping for support, but Mum still made no comment. She had withdrawn from the conversation like a footballer sent off the pitch. She took her mug to the sink and washed it up, then opened the fridge and took out a foil-covered dish.

'Betty Norris saw him in town on Saturday with his new girlfriend,' Nan said. 'It hasn't taken him long.'

Mum straightened up from the oven and turned round quickly as if she were going to swipe something back at Nan. 'Rice or mash with the aubergine bake?' And she smiled, a tight, almost fierce smile that didn't deceive Jo at all.

Twiglets at Break

'She just doesn't *understand*,' Jo grumbled, sitting on a radiator with Lynette at morning break. 'She will keep going on about Dad, as if it's some sort of contest between him and Mum, and he's winning. *Mum* never talks about Dad like that. In fact she hardly ever talks about him at all.'

Lynette poked a straw into the farthest corner of a juice carton and sucked up the last few drops, noisily. She kept a careful eye on the swing doors to the next stretch of corridor. You weren't supposed to eat or drink in the corridors, only in form rooms or outside. But it was far too dismal to go outside and the form room was too crowded and noisy for private conversations. The radiator opposite the Geography office provided a little island of warmth. Jo and Lynette sat there sharing a packet of Twiglets, with their bottoms and thighs roasting pleasantly. A few teachers went past on their way to the staffroom, but fortunately not their Head of Year, Mrs Reynolds, who would have shooed them outside to get some fresh air. Jo had had quite enough fresh air for one day, battling her way against the cold February wind and coaxing the bike up the last hill, and anyway they were having PE after lunch.

'She sounds a right pain, your nan,' Lynette said. 'You could try telling her to mind her own business.'

'I can't. She doesn't mean to be such a pain. It's her way of sticking up for Mum, really.'

Lynette bit a Twiglet neatly in half. 'All the same, if it *upsets* your Mum—'

'Well, it does. You can tell. She never says anything about Dad when Nan starts, it's like she doesn't even hear, but I think –' Jo frowned at a dog-eared map showing coastal erosion '– I think she secretly hopes they'll get back together again.'

'Bit late for that, isn't it? Now that your dad's got his new house and your mum's moved out to the back of beyond?'

'Mum and I could easily move back in with Dad. And Nan –' Jo had to admit that Nan was a bit of a problem '– Nan could stay on in the flat on her own. Mum would still be going over to the shop every day. After all, Mum and Dad aren't divorced yet.'

Lynette waited for a straggle of Year Sevens to go past, moaning about having been kept in late and missing half of break, then she said, 'But they will be, won't they?'

'Only if neither of them stops it. You can stop a divorce, can't you, till it's actually happened? That's why it all takes quite a long time, in case you change your mind.'

'It's no good if only *one* person changes their mind,' Lynette pointed out.

'Well, no, I suppose not—'

Miss Martindale came clop-clopping along the corridor in her neat shoes, carrying a pile of exercise books. She had been the girls' form tutor last year, but she smiled at them absently as if she'd already forgotten their names. Jo, who had shuffled slightly to the right in order to hide the Twiglets, took one out of the packet when Miss Martindale had gone, and sucked at the end until it went soggy. She had just remembered Dad's new girlfriend. The new girlfriend rather got in the way of her theory that Mum and Dad secretly wanted to get back together.

'Dad's been seen with some woman. A new girlfriend,' she told Lynette.

Lynette's brown eyes widened. 'Yeah? And does your mum know?'

'Nan told her. Typical Nan. Couldn't keep a juicy piece of gossip like that to herself, could she?'

'What's she like? The girlfriend?'

'Nan didn't say. She was only passing on what someone else said.' A horrible thought struck her. 'I suppose I might meet her next week, when I'm staying at Dad's. She might even have *moved in*—'

'He might move her out again, as you're coming,' Lynette suggested.

'But if she's around, I *want* to *know*. I bet she's awful. *Girl*friend. I bet she's twenty years younger than him.'

Lynette giggled. 'That would make her nearer your age than his.'

'All the same. That's the sort of thing that happens.'

The Girlfriend walked into Jo's head, smiling triumphantly. She was blonde and busty, about twenty-five, wearing a short skirt and skimpy sweater. She sat down on a chair that conveniently appeared beside her, crossed her legs, twiddled a strand of hair with one finger, and smiled in a provocative sort of way, a smile that said *I've got him now*. Next to her, looking drab and middle-aged, Mum materialised. A bit dumpy, wearing the flat shoes, long skirt and baggy cardigan she usually wore, with tissues bulging the cardigan pockets. Straight brown hair, like Jo's, that she hadn't had time to brush since the morning; a hasty smudge of eye make-up. Wooden beads and earrings, a half-hearted attempt at making herself look attractive. Her face was tired, beginning to droop into resignation. 'Move over. Make way for me,' the Girlfriend said.

'It's not fair,' Jo said aloud.

'What's not fair?' Lynette rummaged in the packet for the last Twiglet fragments.

'That she can come along, all blonde and smug, and pinch my dad. There must be blokes her own age she could have. Why does she bother with Dad?'

Lynette looked puzzled. 'I thought you didn't know what she was like?'

'I don't,' Jo mumbled. 'I was just imagining.'

'Come on, then. Let's go to History before the rush starts.'

They had a new History teacher this term. The one they'd started with, Mr Wishart, had left suddenly last term (Natalie Bayliss boasted that she'd got rid of him), and they'd had no proper teacher at all for a while, just a succession of different people sitting in with them. This term, Miss Kelland had arrived. She was youngish, fashion-conscious and blonde – not unlike the fictitious girlfriend Jo had pictured – and very easy-going. Almost *too* easy-going, Jo thought. Her lessons weren't at all demanding and in fact nobody did much work – Miss Kelland tended to hand out the textbooks and then leave it up to individuals whether they did what she said or not, and she usually forgot to set homework. Mr Wishart had had awful problems trying to keep the class in order but there was no doubt that he knew about History. With Miss Kelland, Jo sometimes wondered. She was often quite happy to wander round the room chatting to people about what they did out of school, and when you handed your book in to be marked she'd just put a tick and *Good*, or *Neat work*. She somehow didn't strike Jo as being a proper teacher; after all, anyone could hand out the books and tell you what page to read. People like Judith and Samantha did pages and pages of neat writing, charts and diagrams, while the middling sort of people like Jo and Amanda and Lynette did what was required and sometimes a nice picture. The really lazy people – mainly boys – did hardly anything.

'Read the two pages about the Civil War and then answer the questions in your books,' Miss Kelland said at the start of the lesson. Mr Wishart would have *told* them about the Civil War, with lots of stories and detail – if people had listened for long enough to let him. But after all the trouble Natalie had stirred up, it was rumoured that Mr Wishart had given up teaching altogether.

Today, Nathan Fuller was in one of his moods. You never knew what to expect with Nathan. Most days, he kept his head low, even if he did little work. But sometimes he'd be in a strange, flippant mood, as if he wanted to get into trouble. This time he'd brought a football with him and put it under his desk, where he kept pushing it with his feet so that it rolled against the legs of the people in front.

'Come on, Nathan,' Miss Kelland said, good-naturedly, after Jason and Sanjay had turned round for the third time to complain.

''S my football,' Nathan said loudly. 'I'll kick it if I want.'

Miss Kelland walked down the row towards him. 'Come on. You'd better give it to me to look after till the end of the lesson.'

'You're not having it.' Nathan was defensive, gearing up for a fight. Everyone watched with wary interest. It was rare for anyone to bother playing up in Miss Kelland's lessons, even the silliest boys like Reado and Damien. It was hardly worth it, as she took so little notice. Most of the boys liked her because she was quite glamorous for a teacher and because she let them joke with her; the girls liked being able to work together and talk throughout the lessons.

'Come on. Pass it over,' Miss Kelland said, smiling.

There was a bit of a struggle, Miss Kelland bending over in her tight short skirt and getting a wolf-whistle from Damien, Nathan grabbing at the ball, and Miss

Kelland finally winning, standing triumphant with the football in her hands.

She still wasn't going to get annoyed. 'You can collect it from me at the end. If you ask politely I won't tell Mrs Reynolds.'

'Tell her if you want. I don't care.' Nathan stood up, defiant. He was a tall skinny boy, with straight dark hair that flopped over his forehead. Underneath his anger, Jo could see that he was tense, shaking, as if his face might crumple into tears. He was trying to act like a hard sixteen-year-old, but was convincing no one.

'Yeah, go on, Nathe. You tell her.' That was Natalie Bayliss, who was always stirring things up.

'Sit down, Nathan. Don't be an idiot,' someone else said. But Nathan had got himself into the centre of attention now, and couldn't back down.

'She can do what she likes. I don't care. I'm not staying anyway. This lesson's rubbish.' He kicked his chair against the wall, pushed past Eduardo and marched out, slamming the door.

For a moment, Miss Kelland looked uncertain. She stood holding the ball, as if unsure whether to run after Nathan or leave him. Then she put the football on top of her filing cabinet, shrugged, and started talking to Samantha as if nothing had happened.

Jo and Lynette exchanged glances, and Lynette

whispered, 'What's up with him?'

'He went to see his dad at the weekend. Greg told me.'

'Why does that make him go off his head?'

'He only sees him three or four times a year. It always puts him in a strop.'

'He's daft if he thinks he can get away with walking out like that. Mrs Reynolds'll be after him later. If Miss Kelland bothers to tell her, that is. Any other teacher would.'

'He's always on report,' Jo said, doodling a picture of a Roundhead in the margin of her exercise book. 'Doesn't make any difference.'

'If you or I barged out like that or kicked footballs in the lesson, just imagine what would happen. He gets away with an awful lot.'

'They make allowances for Nathan. It must be hard for him.'

'Well, it's no harder than for— Have you done question five yet?'

Jo knew that Lynette had been about to say *for you*. Jo's family situation was now the same as Nathan's, except that she saw her father more often. No one made allowances for Jo, as far as she was aware. But then throwing tantrums and stomping about wasn't her way of coping with things. Jo never got into trouble at school. Somehow, her appearance helped; being small and neat, with a face that could look misleadingly angelic, she could get away with all sorts of things that teachers never noticed. She was clever enough not to make it obvious if she was reading a magazine under the table or passing a note to Lynette or doing homework for another teacher. From what they said at parents' evenings and on reports, all her teachers knew her as a lively but well-behaved girl, not a swot like Samantha but not stupid either. They didn't need to know anything had changed. Mr Kershaw knew about her parents splitting up and so, presumably, did Mrs Reynolds, but none of the other teachers needed to. It would only make it worse, if everyone knew. They'd all be discussing your latest mood and waiting to see if you were going to blow a fuse.

During quiet moments in netball after lunch, Jo found herself reconsidering her idea of Mum and Dad getting back together. Was there really any point in hoping? She was playing Goal Attack, her favourite position, but the ball spent most of its time at the other end of the court and Jo was left with Natalie Bayliss, reluctantly playing Goal Defence for the other side, who kept whingeing about having to be outside in the cold. Jo didn't have much time for Natalie, who could always find something to grumble about. She was thinking about how awful it had been at home during the weeks leading up to the separation, and whether it would be like that again. She thought of all the nights she had lain in bed trying not to hear the arguments going on downstairs, but unable to help listening. She had tried to ignore the fact that Mum had moved into the poky spare bedroom – neither Mum nor Dad had ever referred to it. She had tried to pretend that nothing was seriously wrong when Dad had stormed out of the house at ten o'clock at night – where did he *go*? – and when Mum went about her routines with a terrible fragile brightness. Lynette had always said not to worry, because her parents were always arguing, in a cheerful, noisy way, calling each other names and sometimes even throwing things, but it never meant anything; it was a kind of pantomime with them. This had been different. Jo's parents had often gone for two or three days at a time hardly saying anything to each other at all, and that had been far worse. Jo had sometimes thought that if one of them didn't leave home soon, she'd have to go herself. Would it be like that again? Or had Mum discovered that she wanted Dad after all? And would it be any use if she had, now that Dad had met this other—

'Jo! Wake up!'

It was Lynette, playing Centre, about to pass to her. The ball came towards her, straight and fast, and

Natalie made ineffectual jigging and waving gestures as Jo jumped forward and caught it neatly. She pivoted and aimed, all in one movement, right from the edge of the circle, and the ball made a beautiful sure arc, dropping through the net without even seeming to touch the ring.

'Yessss!' Lynette leaped and twisted, punching the air like a footballer, and then gave Jo a thumbs-up and a huge grin.

'Brilliant, Jo!' called Amanda from the centre.

Pride glowed through Jo's whole body. It wasn't uncommon for her to score – she played Goal Attack in the interform competition – but this had been a particularly good goal. Watching that lovely looping shot drawn to the net had been like watching a slow-motion replay – she had known her aim was true, the ball heading for the net as if drawn by a powerful magnet. They were still 4-2 down, because Samantha Warburton was Wing Attack for the other side and she played for the under-sixteen team, but Jo began to take more interest in the game.

Afterwards, when she came out of the girls' changing room, Mr Kershaw was standing by the door opposite to chivvy the boys out of theirs.

'Oh, Jo,' he called to her, 'you won't forget that return slip, will you? For the Outdoor Pursuits trip? I've got to have all the names in by tomorrow.

Thought you'd have wanted to be first in the draw,' he added smiling.

Jo couldn't smile back. 'Forgot,' she mumbled.

Somehow, in spite of the three-way dispute last night, the reply slip had ended up in Mum's tattered folder of Things To Be Done, still not signed.

At Dad's

'I don't know why you don't come out with my ramblers, since you're so keen on keeping fit,' Nan said, wielding a shoe-brush.

It was Sunday morning. Jo had just come in from running, and Nan was polishing her walking boots, which were already perfectly clean as far as Jo could see. She went out every Sunday with the local Ramblers as her weekly exercise. Jo would have found this incongruous – neat, fastidious Nan walking out across muddy fields and climbing over stiles – if it weren't for the fact that Nan put so much effort into turning herself out spotlessly every week, in colour-co-ordinated walking gear, royal blue Gore-tex and Lycra, accessorised with a scarlet headband or, in really cold weather, a blue-and-turquoise fleece hat. Even her bootlaces were royal blue, and she washed them every week as soon as she came in.

'Can't, can I?' Jo said. As if she wanted to. 'I'm going to Dad's.'

'I'm getting an early lunch for you and me, Jo,' Mum said. 'Don't forget we told Dad you'd be there for four.'

Jo was hardly likely to forget. It was her first visit to Dad since he'd moved house, and visits to Dad were planned with military precision by all concerned. Her bags for the week were already packed – a major feat, since it meant thinking of everything she might need for a whole week of school – and Dad would collect them later. Jo was to ride over on the mountain bike.

She made sure she'd left before Dad arrived in his car, and he overtook her on the by-pass, hooting and waving and making a thumbs-up sign about the bike. Jo hated being around when Mum and Dad met each other, which they only ever did from necessity: they were both unnaturally polite, but with enough underlying spikiness to make the air bristle. Jo's other reason for getting herself well out of the way – which, she was fully aware, contradicted her first reason – was that she wanted to leave them alone together. Without her there, Mum might ask Dad in for a cup of tea and they could have a proper conversation, not just about practical arrangements.

However, Dad passed her again, driving away from

Beckley, after an interval so short that he couldn't have spent more than two minutes in the flat. Not a good sign.

Jo had to admit that the mountain bike was fantastic to ride. Once she'd got used to the number of gears and the saddle position, it felt like riding a racehorse after plodding along on a tubby pony. It made nothing of the hill up to Farthingfield, and soared exhilaratingly down the other side. As Jo approached the outskirts of Hagley Heath and found her way into the new housing estate where Dad lived now, she found herself slowing down. For more reasons than one.

Bracken Leas. A name full of whimsy and roses-round-the-door. House builders obviously thought that a picturesquely rustic name somehow made up for the destruction of the environment. The small estate had been built only recently, on a site where Jo remembered a dilapidated Georgian house with a large garden. There was a smart show house at the entrance to the main road and some of the houses were still unoccupied.

Jo saw at once that Dad had made a step up by moving here, half a mile away from the road of identical semis they had lived in before. The new houses were all detached, with their own garages adjoining, and each was different in style from the others: Dad's had a porch with double doors, and bay windows on either side. There was a neatly turfed front garden, no plants in it yet.

Two cars parked outside, she noticed at once. That must mean the new girlfriend was here. Her stomach churned with nervousness and anticipation as she pushed her bike past the parked cars and leaned it against the porch.

Dad had been living in their old house until a fortnight ago. When Jo thought of the old place – the house she had lived in since a baby – being invaded by other people, she felt as if something priceless had been taken away from her. Her childhood had taken place in and around that house. Now she felt as grudging as the Three Bears at the thought of new people sleeping in her bedroom, cooking in the kitchen, reading in the garden. She had seen the new buyers once, just before she and Mum had moved out to the flat. Mr and Mrs Happy Family, with a boy and a girl of primary-school age. They were all cheerful and nice to each other, and enthusiastic about the house and garden. The father had draped his arm around his wife's shoulders as they looked around. Their ideal-family contentment had seemed tactless.

Jo rang the doorbell, which chimed elegantly. Dad, wearing an Aran sweater Mum had knitted for him, opened the door.

'Hi! Where's your bike?'

Jo was staring so hard at the sweater that she almost forgot to answer. It didn't seem right for Dad to wear that, as if nothing had happened.

'Oh – by the porch.'

'We'll put it in the garage. It'll be safer there and anyway it might rain. I'll get the key. I'm not quite straight yet, you'll see. It takes a while…'

You'd think he was afraid of the silence if he stopped talking, Jo thought. He opened the garage door and she wheeled the bike in. There were packing cases inside and some tins of paint laid out carefully on newspapers, a paint-tray with a high-tide mark of cream paint, brushes soaking in a jar.

'Better than that old rattletrap you've been used to, eh?' Dad said, nudging the bike to make sure it wouldn't fall over. 'It must make your ride to school a lot easier?'

'It's great. Thanks.' Jo didn't want to admit that she hadn't yet ridden the new bike to school.

Dad hugged her, now that she didn't have both hands full of bike. 'How's my girl, then?'

'Fine, thanks.' It was what he had always called her. Jo wasn't sure that she *was* his girl any more, not in the same way. Perhaps she was only Mum's girl now. Dad had her on loan occasionally, like a library book. It felt odd, being with Dad. She looked at him with a sense of seeing him for the first time. He was quite good-looking for a dad: thin face, very blue eyes (Jo got her brown ones from Mum), dark hair going a little grey at the edges in a way that quite suited him. He looked so familiar, yet there was a new strangeness between them, especially here, in the house that was Dad's but not Mum's or Jo's. Leaving the old house had been a cutting adrift from the old life, making the split more definite. While Dad had still been there, there had been a chance of going back, but now they had all launched themselves into new lives: Mum and Dad in their separate places, with Jo ferrying back and forth in between. Without me, she thought, they needn't have any more to do with each other. The thought alarmed her. It made her role so important.

Dad opened an interior door and led the way through a utility room (Mum would have loved one of those) and into a fitted kitchen. The house smelled new. Inside, it wasn't all that big, but everything Jo could see – cupboards, cooker, tiled surrounds – was clean and neat, unlike the flat where nothing was quite right or up to date.

'Like it?' Dad put his arm round her shoulders so that they were both facing the garden, a fenced square laid to grass, with a frail-looking tree staked up in one corner. 'I'm not much of a gardener but we'll soon have this planted up and looking like something. How about this kitchen? I chose this pine stuff when I bought the house. It's enough to make Delia Smith jealous, isn't it? A bit smarter than we had at the old place.'

Jo ignored his reference to the old house; she didn't think he should talk about it like that. She wasn't sure, either, whether she liked his arm resting on her shoulders. In one way, she wanted to lean against him and be his little girl, and for him to be good old Dad, the dad he had always been. In another way, she wanted him to acknowledge that things were different now, a bit strained, instead of behaving as if everything was as usual.

'What kind of tree is that?' she asked.

'God, I don't know. It was already here. Let me get you a drink. What would you like? Coke?'

He had already put out glasses on a tray. Three glasses.

'Who else is here?' Jo asked.

'Helen. She's upstairs. Come up and meet her.'

Upstairs?

Jo gave Dad a reproachful look, but he had moved away from her to delve in the fridge for drinks, and didn't notice.

'Helen's an interior designer,' he explained. 'She's just finishing your room.'

Oh. Jo's brain raced to assimilate several new thoughts. Did that mean Helen wasn't Dad's girlfriend after all, just someone who made curtains and things for a job? *Your room*. Jo was to have a room of her own, here in Dad's house, as if she belonged here. A room put together by an interior designer. It sounded very up-market, not the sort of thing she'd have associated with Dad. And very expensive. This very afternoon, Mum was going to shorten an old pair of curtains for Jo's room in the flat. Two people were sorting out bedrooms for her on the same Sunday afternoon. Mum hadn't had much of a weekend break, after working in the shop yesterday and testing new organic dishes this morning. It wasn't fair. Mum couldn't pay for an interior designer.

Dad poured Coke into one glass, beer into the second, and Aqua Libra into the third. 'Come on. We'll take these up and see how she's getting on.' Carrying the tray, he led the way through the main room, which still had packing cases in it, a new-smelling carpet and not much else. Jo followed. Halfway up the stairs it occurred to her that it was a bit odd for an interior designer to be working in someone else's house on a Sunday afternoon. Her first idea must have been right after all.

'Here's Helen,' Dad said on the landing. He put the

tray down on the floor. 'Helen, here's Jo.'

Helen was standing on a chair, hanging a curtain. She immediately jumped down, came towards Jo and shook hands, as if Jo were another adult. She had long dark hair pulled back from her face and wore no make-up. She looked confident and friendly, as if she were genuinely pleased Jo had come. A slim body in denim jeans and a baggy black polo sweater, with some blue threads from the curtain material sticking to the wool. Pretty, without being strikingly so – neat features, blue-grey eyes, a mouth that looked as if it did a lot of smiling.

'I did hope to have your room all ready by the time you came.' She stepped to one side so that the room was displayed. 'But I haven't quite managed it.'

Dad handed her the glass of Aqua Libra. 'What do you think?' he asked Jo.

The curtain Helen had been hanging drooped off its rail, but apart from that the room did look finished. The walls were plain, painted in the palest of mauvy-blues, a colour repeated more boldly in the block-print design of the curtains and duvet. The carpet was new and springy, and there was a bed and desk all-in-one arrangement, the sort Jo had seen in friends' rooms and always wanted – the bed at top bunk height with a ladder up, the desk at right-angles to it, with a hanging space and bookshelves under the bed. The desk had an adjustable reading lamp, a holder for pens and pencils, and three drawers.

'I hate to mention it, but I thought you'd need somewhere to do your homework,' Helen said.

There was a big cork noticeboard along the whole of one wall. Helen hadn't actually gone as far as deciding which posters to put up. As soon as she thought this, Jo felt mean – Helen had obviously put a lot of thought into arranging this room, and had done a good job, considering that she'd never met Jo. There was even a portable TV, on a shelf the same height as the bed, and a mini hi-fi. It could have come straight from the Ideal Home Exhibition or a glossy magazine.

'Thank you. It's great,' Jo said.

As with the bike, she felt that something was stopping her from being quite as grateful as she ought to be. Her voice came out sounding flat, insincere. Dad and Helen probably expected a rapturous response. Perhaps she ought to rush up the little ladder and bounce on the bed, to please them.

It was too easy for Dad. He could simply pay for all this, get someone in and have it done instantly. Mum would sitting there at home, right this minute, toiling away with her temperamental sewing-machine, straining her eyes as she tried to rethread the needle and cope with the obstinate bobbin that kept jumping out, to alter some faded old curtains that were being recycled from the lounge of the old house.

'Do you like it, then?' Dad prompted. 'I thought these bed arrangements were great. Nearly bought one for myself.'

'It's lovely,' Jo said. Again she could hear how hollow her voice sounded. But the room really *was* lovely. If Helen had consulted her at every stage she could hardly have done better. All it needed was posters on the board and some of Jo's own things spread around to make it look really lived-in.

But Jo wasn't going to live here. She was just going to stay, like a guest, for one week in four, or whatever Mum and Dad's latest arrangement was. It was a waste of a room; someone else might as well move in. Jo thought of people sleeping in cardboard boxes because they didn't have anywhere to go, while she had two rooms of her own, now. But this wasn't really hers. Her real room was in Mum's flat.

The thought flashed into her mind that Dad was trying to buy her. The way he had tried with the mountain bike.

It wasn't fair.

It wasn't fair.

Money

'So how's it going then?' Lynette asked at lunchtime. 'With your dad?'

Jo speared a last baked bean. 'All right. I suppose.'

They had been in separate lessons all morning, as well as having Assembly, so there had been no chance to talk; and for the few minutes she had been in the form room Jo had been fobbing off excited questions from the boys about the mountain bike. She had deliberately left Dad's a bit early, in the hope of sneaking into school without attracting attention, but unfortunately Damien had arrived early too and had lost no time in spreading the news of Jo's updated mode of transport. She faced a barrage of questions until Mr Kershaw came in: 'Who on earth lent you *that*, Joke?' 'Can you ride it? I'd have thought your legs were too short to reach the pedals,' and 'Where did you nick it from?' All Jo would say in response was, 'Fairy godmother' – which was true in a way.

Dad did seem to be casting himself as fairy godmother these days.

Lynette already knew about the mountain bike, and was far more interested in Jo's dad. 'You could *tell* me, you mean thing! I'm dying to know about the girlfriend. Was she there?'

'Well. Yes. But first, you'll never guess who lives just round the corner, in one of those posh houses in Dorset Road? Who Dad expects me to be friends with, just because we're in the same form?'

'I don't know.' Lynette looked around the canteen for inspiration. 'Reado? Sanjay? Who?'

'*Natalie*. Natalie I'm-so-cool Bayliss.'

Lynette giggled. 'Don't worry, she's not likely to bother with you. She thinks she's in the sixth form already, the way she swans about.'

'And anyway I've got my bike, so there's no chance of me bumping into her on the corner and having to walk to school with her. Fortunately.'

'She wouldn't *walk* to school,' Lynette said scornfully, 'not *Natalie*. Not now she's got a boyfriend in the Upper Sixth, with a car. If you ask me, the car was the biggest attraction. Don't look now, but she's just come in. With Him.'

Jo felt no inclination to turn and stare. The sight of Natalie and her boyfriend parading each other around like trophies was no novelty. Anything that kept Natalie away from the form room at breaks and lunchtimes was a good thing, as far as Jo was concerned. A few moments later, Natalie and the boy, Darren, came into her field of vision, carrying trays from the serving hatch. They went directly to the only free table, put down their trays and sat very close together, whispering and giggling.

'You'd think a sixth-form boy would get the mickey taken for cradle-snatching, going around with a girl from Year Nine,' Lynette said, opening a carton of yoghurt.

'Natalie doesn't look like Year Nine. You'd think she was older than him,' Jo said. She considered Darren Hobson to be a pathetic specimen – good-looking, flashy, but completely vacant, as far as she could tell. He was one of the more conspicuous older boys around the campus, fond of posing by the railings outside the main doors at breaks and lunchtimes, where the girls coming in got the best view of him.

'At least Natalie doesn't tag along with Amanda and Ellie any more. Anyway, never mind her,' Lynette urged. 'What about your dad's girlfriend?'

'Helen. Well, at first I didn't think she *was* Dad's girlfriend, because she's an interior designer and she was round there doing up my bedroom. It's lovely. But then there was no sign of her going home once she'd done the curtains and later on she went out and got an Indian take-away for us all. We sat on the floor eating it because there's no furniture. Not downstairs, anyway.'

It had been, unexpectedly, fun – perhaps because of sitting on the floor rather than round a table. Dad had set fire to some popadums when he left them under the grill while he looked for mango chutney, and the smoke alarm had gone off. And then Helen had taken too big a mouthful of lime pickle and nearly choked. While she was sipping the glass of water Dad fetched for her and gasping that her mouth was on fire, a black-and-white cat had strolled into the room and looked at them all in surprise, before bolting out again. 'I left the kitchen window open, because of the burning smell,' Dad said. 'I'll have to make sure I keep it shut in future,' but Helen said immediately, 'Oh, don't. It'd be nice to have a cat. Perhaps he's a stray,' and Jo hadn't been able to help warming to her.

'And? What's she *like?*' Lynette persisted.

'Nice, really. Easy. Not – oh, I don't know – all dressed-up or silly or pleased with herself. Just a nice person. Young*ish*, quite pretty.'

'Does she actually live there? Did she stay the night?' Lynette asked, with raised eyebrows.

'No. She's got a flat of her own near the station.

We're not going to see her again till Wednesday. Dad's got a new job, by the way. Sales Manager. That partly explains where all this money's coming from. It's a much better job than his old one.'

'Sales Manager of what?'

'That new toy shop on the Beckley by-pass, would you believe? Right next to Sainsbury's where we do our shopping. *Toyz World*, it's called – *Toyz* with a Z, that is. What a stupid name. They might as well have gone all the way and called it *Toyz 4 Kidz*.'

That was another difficulty. She had scorned the new toy store often enough – for being brash and new, for having a stupid name, and for making the small toy shop in the High Street close down. Now *Toyz World* was paying for her mountain bike, her bedroom, the Indian take-away meal, everything that came from Dad.

'You mean to say your dad's working just down the road from your mum?'

'That's right. So close they could see each other every lunchtime if they wanted to.' Or Dad could go into Mum's shop to buy health food for lunch and give her some business, Jo thought, if he really wanted to do her a favour. But Dad was sceptical about health food, and he probably didn't want to see Mum anyway. Jo wasn't sure whether Mum knew about the job yet, or how she'd feel if she did.

It made it worse, somehow, the fact that they were working so close but ignoring each other. It would have been better, Jo thought, if she and Mum could have moved a hundred miles away instead of ten minutes' drive from Dad. It would have made more of a break.

'Even if this Helen is nice,' Lynette said, 'she gets in the way a bit, doesn't she? Of your plan to get your mum and dad back together?'

'Yes. She does.' Jo fiddled with an apple core, flicking the pips on to her plate. 'It's not really a plan, just an idea, and a pretty stupid one. Now I won't know how much to tell Mum about Helen when I go back home. I'll have to say something, won't I? Otherwise I'll be – kind of siding with Dad. Keeping a secret.'

'It's not a secret. Your nan knew about it, let alone your mum. Your mum may as well know.' Lynette scraped her spoon round her yoghurt carton. 'The only answer is for her to get a boyfriend. Then it won't matter.'

'What, *Mum?*'

'Don't gawp at me like I'm from outer space. It's not such a crazy idea, is it? She's not that old. Things like that happen.'

'Not to Mum,' Jo said. 'She hasn't got time.'

*

Jo was glad that Helen wasn't going to be at Dad's house that night. Perhaps, in a way, Helen's presence had made things easier at first, but it had made it very hard to talk about Mum and the shop – *even* to *mention* Mum. It was as if Mum had become a taboo subject. Jo felt that she had to obey the rules of a new game, without anyone actually explaining them to her. Mum had gone from Dad's life and Helen had arrived instead. But it didn't seem right for them all to pretend Mum had been zapped out of existence by a passing alien.

Tonight, Jo thought, I shall talk about Mum. Dad ought to be interested in how she's getting on, anyway. About the shop, and the flat, and what she does at weekends. He ought to know how hard she works.

She wasn't sure what Dad was planning to do about food; he'd never done much cooking when they all lived together and she couldn't imagine him starting now. He hadn't mentioned it, otherwise she could have peeled potatoes or something. She finished her homework before he came in and was wondering whether to go out for a run – the bike ride to and from school wasn't enough to keep her fit – but then Dad might come in and wonder where she was. It would be easier to watch *Neighbours*, and go for a run later, when Dad was here. Somehow, with no one else in the house, she felt strange, as if she didn't really have a right to be here. Hungry when she came in, she had looked in the kitchen cupboards for biscuits and had felt like a thief, even though she hadn't found any.

When Dad came in, he was carrying two Sainsbury's bags, which he unloaded on one of the kitchen work-surfaces. 'Chicken pies, oven chips, peas, ice-cream. That OK?'

'Fine,' Jo said.

It wasn't the sort of thing they ever had at home. Mum would have pointed out that chickens reared for pies lived unnatural lives in broiler houses, had an artificial diet and were slaughtered on production lines at a few weeks old. Jo could hear Mum's voice in her head. She didn't like the idea any more than Mum did, but it wasn't the moment for a discussion on the rights and wrongs of factory farming.

Dad kissed her. 'Get the kettle on, there's my girl. Let's have some tea. I'll get the oven on.'

He was wearing a dark grey suit with a badge on the lapel, which had the *Toyz World* logo and *Richard Cannon: Sales Manager.* The suit made him look like someone who worked in a bank or an office; the red-and-blue teddy-bear logo looked ridiculous against it.

'Did you wear that badge in Sainsbury's?' Jo asked.

She wondered whether people would have seen it and giggled at him for being a teddy-bear salesman. It could be worse, though. The toy store could have him dressed up as Donald Duck or Superman. He might sell more toys that way.

Dad's hand went to his lapel. 'Forgot all about it. Haven't got used to wearing it yet.'

He went upstairs to change, and came down looking less like a funeral director and more like Dad. They ate their meal sitting on cushions on the new carpet in the lounge, as they had the night before when Helen was there.

'So how's your mum getting on with the shop?' Dad asked.

Jo looked at him. It was the first time he'd asked directly about Mum. If he wanted to know, he could have asked Mum herself when he went over for Jo's bags yesterday afternoon.

'All right. It's hard work. She's always cooking things to sell, you know, the packaged meals. But she never seems to get many customers.'

Dad shook his head. 'I'm not surprised. It's a quiet little backwater, Beckley. Steff ought to have gone for Milton Keynes, or here.'

'She couldn't pay the rent. Beckley was all she could afford.'

'I know. But she needs to make a go of it. Sometimes

you need to spend money to make money.'

'But how, if you haven't *got* money to start with?' Jo swallowed a mouthful of chicken pie, trying not to think of broiler chickens being stuffed into crates and then hauled out by slaughtermen. There was a chicken processing plant on the Beckley by-pass – on the opposite side of town from Sainsbury's and *Toyz World*, where people didn't have to see it or think about it, or smell the burning of chicken waste. Jo passed the lorries going there nearly every day on her way to school, bringing chickens from the farms – she could see white feathers protruding from the crates. The taste of chicken in her mouth was sickening, smooth and bland in its coating of sauce, like processed rubber. She pushed the rest of her pie aside, deciding to stick to the chips and peas.

'Anyway, she *is* making a go of it,' she said. 'She'll be devastated if it all folds up.'

She didn't like admitting the possibility. If Mum's shop *did* fold up – first her marriage and then her shop – what would be left for her?

'It was a gamble. Steff knew that,' Dad said. 'I pointed out the risks when she insisted on going ahead with it. Small businesses fold up every day. You've only got to look at the High Street here. Little shops like that are changing hands all the time. Clothes shops, food shops, bookshops – they can't compete with the big companies.'

'So you don't think Mum ought to have started up, then?' Jo couldn't eat any more. She put her plate down on the carpet and waited for Dad to finish.

'It's what she wanted. Your nan was keen to help, and she had some savings of her own. I put mine into this house. But if you ask me,' Dad said, scraping up the last smears of sauce, 'she'd have done better to stick with her old job. You're lucky if you've got a secure job these days – she might find it hard to get another one. Her trouble was she never really made the best of herself – never bothered to get any proper qualifications. Never thought it was worth it, as long as she had that office job. Anyway, how are you getting on with your nan, in that little flat? She'd drive me up the wall, I have to say.' He gave Jo a small, mischievous grin, as if Nan's irritatingness was a secret they could share.

'Nan's all right,' Jo said promptly. It was one thing for *her* to criticise Nan, quite another for Dad to start weighing in. Nan was Mum's mum, not his. She was nothing to do with him any more.

Jo collected the plates together and went out into the kitchen to get the ice-cream. She seemed to spend all her time at home defending one member of the family against another, like a one-person peacekeeping force.

*

Ellie Byrne rushed up next morning while Jo was locking up her bike. 'Jo! Jo!'

Ellie wasn't much given to running about excitedly; something catastrophic must have happened.

'The list's gone up,' Ellie panted.

'What list?'

'You know! The list for the Outdoor Pursuits week – you're on it!'

Jo stared at her. 'How can I be? I didn't even bring the form back!'

'Well, your name's there. So's mine.'

'It must be a mistake, then. My name didn't go in the hat.'

Mystified, Jo shouldered her rucksack and followed Ellie towards the noticeboard outside the Year Nine office. An excited group, mainly boys pushing and shoving each other and shouting out names, blocked Jo's view of the board so that she had to stand on tiptoe and crane her neck. OUTDOOR ACTIVITIES WEEK – PENHOWELL, the notice said, and – a quick sidestep to the right to avoid being barged aside by the bag slung over Reado's shoulder – there it was, JO CANNON, the third name on the list, after ELENA BYRNE.

'And Lynette!' Jo said. Lynette wasn't here yet, as she always dropped off her twin brothers at the primary school first. 'She'll be pleased. But,' she told Ellie, 'I didn't even give Mr Kershaw the bit of paper! He asked me for it twice and then he forgot.'

'Amanda hasn't got a place – she doesn't know yet and she's going to be really gutted.' Ellie gave her a doubtful look. 'I was going to ask if I could share a room with you and Lynette.'

'There's going to be another place spare, then. Mine. Amanda can have that.'

Ellie looked doubtful. 'Don't you *want* to go?'

'Yes, I do! I really do, but I didn't put my name in because we can't afford it. Not just after moving and – and all that.'

'Oh, right. That's tough.' Ellie knew enough about Jo's home situation to be able to sympathise.

'I mean, this is a bit much,' Jo said feelingly. 'I've got over the disappointment *once*, when we first heard about it – deciding I wouldn't be able to go. Now I've got to go through it again, getting my name taken off the list.'

'Well, they have a special fund, don't they?' Ellie suggested. 'So that people who – I mean, to make it fair, so that people don't have to miss out on things just because they—'

'I know what you mean. Hardship fund, they call it. But I don't think Mum and I exactly come into that category, not yet anyway.'

'No, sorry. I didn't mean—' Ellie bit her lip, her face anxious. 'I just thought it would be a shame for you not to go if you really want to. Now that you've got a place.'

'It's OK.' Jo smiled, to show that she hadn't taken offence. She liked Ellie, a quiet, rather serious girl, whose mass of wavy hair and dark eyebrows gave her a dreamy, brooding look, like someone in a painting. Jo didn't think Ellie's parents had money to throw around either. Not like Judith's, who had given Judith a pony as a birthday present, or Natalie's, whose house in Dorset Road was about twice the size of Jo's dad's.

'Perhaps Steve sorted something out without telling you,' Ellie suggested. 'Why don't you ask him?'

'Let's go now. He'll be in the PE office.'

Mr Kershaw – Steve, as most of the form called him except to his face – was coming out of his office with a mug of coffee, dressed as usual in sweatshirt and tracksuit trousers. 'Hi there, Cannonball!' he greeted Jo – this was his own nickname for her, because of her habit of hurtling along corridors and round corners. 'Morning, Elliephant!' (His name for Ellie.) 'Seen your names up on the list?'

'That's what I've come to tell you,' Jo said. 'I can't go. It's a mistake.'

'What do you mean, a mistake?'

'I didn't give you the form back. I don't know how my name came out of the hat, because it never went in it.'

Mr Kershaw looked puzzled. He walked backwards through his office door as if someone had pressed the rewind button on a video player. 'Yes, it did,' he said from inside. 'I've got all the forms here.' He put his coffee mug down and shuffled through a folder. 'Jo Cannonball. Here it is.'

'Let's see! It must be someone messing about!'

Jo took the form he held out. She had last seen it in Mum's kitchen and had believed it to be lost and forgotten, but here it was, with the others and all filled in properly. Signed *Richard Cannon*, in her father's biro scrawl.

Outreach

'Yes, I told Dad about it,' Mum said defensively.

'Why?'

'I knew he'd pay, if I told him about the course. He can afford it. I don't see why you should miss out.'

Jo couldn't miss the miserable twist of Mum's mouth. Mum was sitting at the kitchen table and had been working out her shop accounts for the week while cooking supper; the account book lay closed on the table. The words, 'Well, you could have *told* me,' shrivelled into silence on Jo's lips. The closed book, and Mum's resigned expression, indicated that takings hadn't been good this week. It must be hard for Mum to admit that Dad was the one with the bulging wallet and bottomless chequebook. Dad could give Jo things and smooth out difficulties with the ready flow of his money. Jo had pulled a face at *Toyz World* as she cycled past on her way home. *Toyz World* was paying for the

Outdoor Pursuits trip. *Toyz World* had paid for the mountain bike. *Toyz World* was beginning to feel like her official sponsor.

'Aren't you pleased you're going to Wales?' Mum asked. 'I knew you really wanted to.'

'Oh, yes – yes, I am!' Jo realised that she *could* be pleased, now that it was all settled and both Mum and Dad knew what was going on. 'Thanks, Mum. There's a meeting on Monday and Mr Kershaw's going to tell us all about it. What we'll be doing and what we need to take.'

Nan came into the kitchen in her dressing-gown, in time to overhear. 'Is that friend of yours going? That coloured girl?'

'Lynette. She's black, not coloured.' Jo tried not to grit her teeth. Nan always referred to Lynette as 'that coloured girl,' as if Lynette's non-whiteness was the only thing about her worth mentioning. She could have said, 'that girl with the lovely smile', or 'that girl who's such a good friend to you'. Or even, with a huge effort of memory, 'Lynette'. Nan must have heard the name enough times.

Nan poured herself a cup of Earl Grey. Jo wondered whether she were ill or something, wandering around in her dressing-gown at six o'clock in the evening. But then she'd obviously just had her hair done – it had been tinted the colour of pale custard and stiffly blow-dried, so that it looked like a loo brush. Nan wouldn't have gone and had her hair loo-brushed if she wasn't well.

'And how was your week?' she asked Jo.

'Fine, thanks.' Jo did a quick editing job in her head, for Mum's sake. 'We had an Indian take-away on Sunday and I surfed the net on Dad's computer. And he came out running with me, twice.'

Mum looked up with an incredulous expression, and Nan said, 'Running? Your dad?' She huffed a laugh, looking in the biscuit barrel. 'That's a new one.'

Jo noticed that he had become *Your dad* now, not just *Dad*. As if he were some private possession of Jo's, nothing to do with the rest of them. It was the same as Dad referring to Mum as Steff, not Mum any more. 'Well, he doesn't, really,' she said. 'He got a stitch and had to give up. He's awfully unfit.'

'Bone idle, that one,' Nan said.

Jo glanced at Mum, and saw again the lips pressed tightly together, as if she had to prevent a sharp comment escaping. Mum never criticised Dad, and she obviously didn't like it when Nan did. Any minute now, Jo thought, and Nan will ask about the new girlfriend – the soul of tact, as ever. Jo wasn't going to say anything about Helen, about the luxurious new bedroom, about how smug Dad was with his new job and his new life – not at all if she could help it, and certainly not when Nan was around. It was easier to carry on talking about the running. She plunged on, 'I ran every night, even when Dad didn't come. You only have to cross the main road and then you can get into the park and run along by the canalside. It makes quite a good circuit.'

'I hope you didn't go down by the canal when it was dark,' Mum said. She got up and took knives and forks from the drawer, and laid two places, with a sort of careful nonchalance. Jo could tell she was dying to hear more about Dad, but didn't want to ask.

'No, I didn't,' Jo said, although she had once, and had found it a bit scary – after all, you never knew what maniac you might find lurking under one of the bridges, waiting for someone to push in. 'And Lynette came with me, once.'

'Why does your dad want to get fit, all of a sudden? He never bothered before,' Nan said, acidly.

'I don't know.' Jo had a sneaking idea that it was something to do with Helen – Dad wanting to look young and streamlined, rather than almost middle-aged which he actually was – but she could hardly say so. It would be insulting to Mum to imply that Dad as an idle slob had been good enough for her, but that

Helen deserved better. 'Mum, you've only laid two places,' she said. ' I'm home now, remember?'

'Can't stand here chatting,' Nan said. 'Time's getting on. I must go and make myself look beautiful.' She went out with her cup and saucer, and a moment later Jo heard the bath taps running.

Jo raised her eyebrows, and Mum said, 'Nan's going out tonight, for a meal.'

'Who with?'

'Well, actually—' Mum's tone became furtive, as if she thought Nan might have sneaked back to hide in the larder, listening. 'She's going out with a man she's met, in her Ramblers' group. He sounds quite nice. I've spoken to him on the phone.'

Jo felt her mouth fall open. 'Nan, going out with a *man*! At *her* age! It's in*dec*ent!'

'Don't be ridiculous, Jo. I know you think she's as old as the Ancient Mariner, but there's no reason why she shouldn't have a friend.'

'Yes, but a *man!* What's his name?'

'Dennis,' Mum said.

'Yuk! *Dennis!* I might have guessed it would be that sort of name.'

'Oh? Is there something wrong with the name Dennis? I don't find it objectionable myself.'

'Well, can you think of anyone reasonable who's called Dennis?' Jo lifted the lid of the teapot, inhaled

Earl Grey perfume and decided to do herself a tea-bag mug instead. 'Can you think of anyone at all, apart from Dennis the Menace?'

'Dennis Potter, Dennis Healey,' Mum said promptly. 'You shouldn't judge people by their names, even if for some strange reason you find the name Dennis hilarious.'

'And getting her hair done specially! She must be taking it seriously. At *her* age – at least fifty—'

'Fifty-nine, actually. That's not old. I suppose you think I'm over the hill, at thirty-six?' Mum said crisply.

'No! There's a lot of difference between thirty-six and fifty-nine.' All the same, Jo couldn't help looking at Mum rather critically, remembering Lynette's idea about Mum getting a new boyfriend. She couldn't see it happening, herself. It wasn't so much that Mum was a bit dowdy and drab; Mum could make herself look quite reasonable if she wanted to, and when she smiled – which wasn't very often these days – she was at least halfway to being pretty. The problem was that Mum never *went* anywhere. Jo quite liked the idea of Mum finding a New Man. To go out with, just to show Dad: Jo wasn't sure she felt ready to think about step-families just yet, even if there was a possiblity of ending up with a lovely stepbrother like Amanda's Luke. But how was Mum possibly going to meet anyone? The only chance was that the Right Man might just happen to wander into the health shop in search of soya milk or tofu patties. And how likely was that? Mum might wait years. And even if the Right Man did come in, he might simply buy something and go out again, and neither of them would ever know that they'd missed each other. The circumstances would have to be exactly right. Like this:

New Man: *Is this food home-made?*

Mum: (blushing modestly) *Yes. I make it all myself.*

New Man: *Really! What an amazing piece of luck! You see I'm a television producer and I'm desperately searching for someone to present a new series on organic cookery. I suppose you wouldn't be interested?*

Mum: (bashfully) *Oh no, I couldn't possibly. I've never done anything like that before.*

New Man: *Don't worry about that. You'd be a natural, I can tell. Tell you what (looking at watch) – why don't we discuss it over lunch?*

But then even that wouldn't work. If he were a TV producer, he'd be brash and confident, the last sort of man Mum would be attracted to. No, he'd have to be a local bee-keeper or free-range poultry farmer who came into the shop to sell his honey or eggs. That would mean regular contact—

'What?' She realised that Mum had been talking to her.

'I just said,' Mum said in a bristly sort of way, 'that there's not all *that* much difference between my age and Nan's – not as much as you think, anyway. If I'm as fit and active when I'm her age, I shall be extremely pleased. And if you could possible avoid going all giggly and silly when Nan comes back in, I'd appreciate it.'

That wasn't fair! Jo wasn't the giggly type. Mum checked the potato saucepan, and said primly, 'It's quite possible, you know, for people over thirty to have social lives. You shouldn't think your generation knows all about everything.'

'I don't! You've got to admit it's a bit funny, that's all, Nan having a boyfriend.' Mum *had* thought so, Jo could tell from the way she first mentioned it.

'You'd better not call him a boyfriend. Not to Nan. Get the salad dressing out of the fridge, could you? It's in the door.'

Jo bent down to get it, and straightening up noticed

a postcard held up by the fridge magnet. 'Who's this from?' she asked.

'From Stella. Read it if you like.'

The postcard showed a pretty stone village, and the writing said *All going well up here. Lovely place and people very friendly. You must come up and stay some time, Love Stella.* Stella was Mum's best friend, who had just moved away to Yorkshire. Mum seemed to be unlucky in all directions just at the moment. Putting the postcard back under the magnet, Jo saw a printed form lying on top of the fridge, with the questions answered in Mum's handwriting.

'Outreach Courses,' she read. 'What's this, Mum?'

'Oh – I'm joining an evening class. I saw it advertised in the library. Well, not a class as such – more of a reading circle.'

'A what?' The idea of a reading circle made Jo giggle, reminding her of infant school – sitting round in a circle reading *Through the Rainbow Gold Book 4*, then going on to a harder book when you'd finished it and the teacher said you could.

'We meet once a week to discuss books. I went last week to see if I liked it, and now I'm joining properly.'

'What for?'

'Rinse that lettuce, could you, and make the salad? Well, it may surprise you, but I do have a brain, and

I've decided not to let it moulder. We study different writers and different periods of literature. We're starting with Romanticism and then going on to the Victorians.'

'Romanticism? That doesn't sound worth going to a reading circle for. What is it, Barbara Cartland sort of stuff?'

'No. That's Romance. Romanticism is – well, literature from the time of the French Revolution. We're starting off with the *The Rime of the Ancient Mariner*.'

Jo prepared salad, mulling this over. *Outreach Course* – she imagined arms, hands, stretching and reaching out for new knowledge and experiences. Reading books and talking about them didn't sound like a particularly thrilling sort of social life, but at least it meant Mum was doing something that was just for herself, away from the shop and the flat. Perhaps New Man would be there, just waiting for someone like Mum to come along, eagerly thirsting for knowledge! She could see him, bearded and intellectual in a corduroy jacket, leading earnest discussions about the Ancient Mariner.

'Who *is* this Ancient Mariner you keep going on about, anyway?' she asked.

*

Jo was hoping for a glimpse of Dennis, but as soon as the doorbell rang, Nan was off. She grabbed her coat, kissed Jo and Mum quickly – smelling of lily-of-the-valley perfume – and darted downstairs, before anyone else could go. She was wearing a jumper in such a glaring shade of fuchsia pink that Jo hoped Dennis had brought sun-glasses. She had earrings to match, and had fluffed up her hair even more, so that it now resembled a prize chrysanthemum.

'Don't be late back,' Mum teased.

'I won't. But don't wait up.' Nan's voice came up the stairs, all coy and girlish. Even Nan was treating it as a joke, playing at being a sixteen-year-old.

Jo heard a deep male voice, saying something that was cut off by the slamming of the door. Mum went back to reading *Frankenstein* (which, to Jo's surprise, was one of the books for the Romanticism part of her course; Jo had thought it was just a horror film) and Jo flicked restlessly through a magazine. Nan had bought it for her when she went into the newsagent's for her *Woman's Weekly*, which had been kind of her, although Jo rarely bothered to read magazines. Nan must have been deceived by the demurely pretty girl on the front cover, because if she'd looked inside she'd have come over all prim and prudish and When-I-was-your-age. Jo turned the pages. *When Are You Ready for Sex?* was on one page, and *Are You Clued Up About Snogging?* – all the usual stuff. As far as Jo could see, it was people Dad's age and Nan's age who needed to read this sort of thing, not her.

She read some of the problem page letters, for a laugh, and then thought about the new problem waiting in her rucksack. Another letter, demanding attention. She looked at Mum, who was deep in an armchair and totally engrossed in her book, her mouth slightly open, one hand twiddling a strand of hair. It looked like being an exciting Friday evening. Back at the old house, Jo would probably have gone out with Lynette – ice-skating or to the cinema. But the ice-rink and the cinema were miles away. Lynette was coming over for the day tomorrow, but that was tomorrow. Jo almost considered doing her weekend homework to get it out of the way, but being a Sunday evening last-minuter was a hard habit to break. If she'd been at Dad's she could have had got on the computer and e-mailed Lynette, but she crushed that thought as disloyal to Mum – this was home, not Dad's, for better or worse. She turned back through the magazine, pausing at *Ten Ways to Attract Male Glances*. She couldn't care less herself whether males glanced at her or not – why did teenage magazines assume that every girl over the age of ten was obsessed with boys? – but maybe the article would be of use to Mum. Jo read it carefully. Somehow she couldn't see Mum going in for hair-flicking or eyelash-batting or wearing a crop-top and getting her navel pierced (*disgusting!*) and anyway, Dad was the one Mum wanted to attract, or re-attract... Really, it would have been easier if Helen had turned out to be horrible, or a real bimbo. Somehow, Dad had to go off Helen, and realise that Mum was the one he wanted. After all, Mum was doing something to improve herself now, reading all these books and knowing about the Ancient Mariner. The thought niggled Jo that Dad would be more impressed with a Business Studies Diploma or a course in Management Skills, but all the same it was *something*.

Mum reached the end of a chapter and stood up. 'Fancy a coffee?'

'No, thanks. But Mum, there's this letter I need to show you.'

Mum looked wary, as if she suspected more money. 'What letter?'

'There's an Options Evening after half-term. We've got to choose our Options for next year, and everyone's parents have got to come in to meet our form tutor and the Careers Adviser. I'll fetch it.'

'Oh. I see.' Mum frowned. 'Yes, I suppose so. Both parents. This is the first parents' evening, isn't it, since—'

'Yes,' Jo said. 'Since.'

'And an important one. Who do you want to come?' Mum said, looking directly at Jo.

'I don't know.' It was like being asked to make some final, decisive choice. 'You. Or you and Dad. But not just Dad.'

'OK,' Mum said. 'Dad and I ought to go together. I'll ring him.'

Lynette came over on Saturday and they went for a long walk, right down to the lake on the other side of Farthingfield, running for part of the way where the clay wasn't so heavy as to stick to their boots.

'We're not half fit enough,' Jo panted, 'for going up real mountains. The Brecon Beacons. The Black Mountains. Pen y Fan. Corn Du.' She liked saying the names; they were like spells. The map held magic too; she had borrowed one from the Geography Department and pored over it, looking at the brown corrugations of contours, the winding blue threads of mountain streams, the black clustered lines of crags and screes. In a matter of weeks they would materialise as moorland, hillside, ridge.

'I shouldn't worry,' Lynette assured her. 'Half the people going aren't doing anything at all to get fit. If they can do it, we can.'

Jo looked round at the gently sloping fields of the

rural Midlands, and imagined herself in real wild country, with peaks enticing her to the heights, away from roads, away from building sites and towns and shops. She was counting the days.

Options

Half-term was over, and the remaining time between now and the Outdoor Pursuits course had shrunk till it was measurable in terms of weeks and days, rather than months. Jo felt a clutch of excitement at her stomach whenever she thought about it. She could hardly bear to believe that the six days of the course would go at the same speed as other ordinary days, and be processed into the past. Those six days had become the focus of her entire year. She hoped she would be able to cope with all the activities without disgracing herself: she'd heard of people freezing up with fear on rock-faces or getting claustrophobic down pot-holes and having screaming fits or refusing to move. Having a go at anything was a matter of pride for Jo, and she was determined not to give way to fear, no matter what impossible feats she was asked to do.

Half-term was spent partly at Dad's and partly at

home. Lynette and Jo took the twins, Gary and Gavin, to the cinema for a birthday treat. Dad stopped running and took up weight training. Jo helped out in the shop, weighing and labelling packets of nuts and spices, making a new display of cruelty-free cosmetics. Mum read *Frankenstein*, *Mansfield Park* and a lot of poems by Keats, which Jo looked at but found incomprehensible, apart from 'La Belle Dame Sans Merci', which she liked. Nan had no more evenings out with Dennis: 'Perhaps that gruesome pink sweater made his eyes hurt, or else he was knocked out by her sickly perfume,' Jo told Mum. However, Nan and a group of five others from the Ramblers – including Dennis – were planning a walking trip to Norfolk, staying in youth hostels.

'In youth hostels!' Jo exploded, repeating this bit of information to Lynette. They were eating toasted hot cross buns in Lynette's bedroom, where they had escaped from Gary and Gavin and their endless demands for games. 'I thought youth hostels were for youth, not for the over-sixties. They might as well combine them with nursing homes for geriatrics.'

'Your nan's not geriatric,' said Lynette, always fair-minded. 'And for someone who's always going on about chicken rights and human rights and rights of everything down to two-toed sloths in Amazon rainforests, you're pretty ageist, if you ask me.'

'I don't mean to be ageist. It's just Nan.' A trickle of butter escaped down Jo's chin; she tried to lick it off.

'Stop it! You're going cross-eyed.' Lynette stretched an arm to the window-sill and passed Jo a tissue. 'Why shouldn't she go on walking trips? Would you prefer it if she sat by the fire knitting and complaining about her bunions?'

'No,' Jo had to admit. 'But having a boyfriend is a bit much, isn't it?'

'It doesn't sound as if he *is* a boyfriend. Going out once. What about your mum? Has she met anyone interesting at her Frankenstein Club?'

Jo giggled. The Frankenstein Club conjured up visions of Mum and the other members messing about in a dimly-lit laboratory, sewing bits of bodies together and waiting for a thunderstorm. Far more exciting than it actually was – all Mum did these days, when she wasn't cooking or worrying about her accounts, was read and make notes. 'Not that I know of,' Jo said. 'She's met Keats and Jane Austen and Wordsworth, but they're all dead. And all these people who write books about authors, telling you what their books mean. You can't get near the kitchen table for library books these days. And anyway, Mum doesn't really want to meet a new man, if that's what you meant. She wants Dad.

Options Evening!' she announced, remembering. 'That's their chance.'

'I don't see why Options Evening's so special. They see each other fairly often anyway, don't they? When he comes over to collect your bags or bring them back?'

'Yes, but that's all busy and practical. You know, *"What time shall I expect you on Friday?"* and *"Don't forget she's got netball practice on Thursday."* They're always in a hurry. And besides, Nan's always there.'

'So you think the Careers Room is just the romantic setting they need, then?' Lynette raised sceptical eyebrows. 'With Mr Kershaw and Mrs Reynolds there?'

'No, stupid. I mean afterwards. The Options interview's going to take about twenty minutes at the most. We'll most likely go out to a restaurant afterwards. All three of us.'

'Have you told them?'

'Not actually *told* them, no.'

'They're telepathic?' Lynette dabbed a finger at the crumbs on her plate.

Jo shrugged.

'It strikes me,' Lynette says, 'you'd better leave them to sort themselves out. You can't really interfere when you don't know what they want.'

'*They* don't know what they want. They need me to tell them, that's the whole point,' Jo said. 'I wish I had parents like yours, always cheerful. How do they *do* it?' Lynette's father could be heard singing in a high falsetto voice downstairs, while he sandpapered the front-room door.

'I know. It gets on your nerves first thing Monday morning,' Lynette said. 'All this opera. He gets a CD and plays it over and over again in his taxi till he knows it off by heart, and then we get it for days on end. *Madame Butterfly*, this is. It was *The Marriage of Figaro* before that. And you should hear it when the boys join in. The neighbours must think we're running a cats' home.'

When Options Evening came, Jo made every effort to nudge Mum in the right direction. Mum always got nervous about occasions like this, as if it were her future being decided, not Jo's. She started getting agitated as soon as she came up from the shop.

'What do you think I should wear? My suit?' she asked Jo.

God, no. Mum's suit only came out for interviews and funerals; it was dark navy and made her look like a bus-conductor, except when she wore her red, white and blue scarf with it, and then she looked like a stewardess for British Airways. It wasn't at all what

Jo had in mind. She wanted Mum to look her best, not all stiff and formal.

'You don't have to be *smart*,' Jo pointed out. 'Why don't you wear—' Mentally, she roamed around Mum's wardrobe in search of inspiration. 'I know, that lacy jumper, the blue one. Dad—' She bit off the words *Dad likes that*.

'Your dad's bound to look smart. In his office suit. Cut some bread, could you, Jo? There's no time for a proper meal. We'll have beans on toast before we go.'

'Umm, no, thanks. I'm not hungry.'

Mum looked at her suspiciously. Jo was *always* hungry. 'I suppose you're a bit nervous. Do you want to wait till afterwards?'

So far, so good. The next stage would require tact and delicacy. Once she'd got Mum and Dad together in a restaurant (Dad would offer to pay, of course) she'd have to find a way of leaving them alone together. Refuse coffee and then remember she'd promised to phone Lynette? Pretend to have seen someone she knew in the car park? Go to the Ladies and discover she had a zit that needed squeezing? – that sort of thing. Left alone with Dad in the soft candlelight, Mum could tell Dad all about Frankenstein and the Ancient Mariner, and he'd be impressed because she was making something of herself. It would go like this:

Dad: *You've changed, Steff.*

Mum: *Yes, I know. It's been hard but I'm learning how to cope.*

Dad: (gazing wistfully at her) *You don't have to cope on your own, you know.*

Mum: (pretending not to understand) *I'm not on my own. I've got Jo and Mum.*

Dad: *That's not what I mean.* (Softly) *It's not the same without you, Steff. Couldn't we try again? Can't we admit we made a big mistake, splitting up?*

Mum: (trying not to sound too obviously accusing) *WHO made a mistake, did you say?*

Dad: (grovelling a bit): *Well, all right. I made a big mistake. I didn't appreciate what you mean to me, Steff. You and Jo. I still love you, surely you must realise that?*

Mum: (a bit of hair flicking and eyelash-batting would fit in well here) *Do you really? Oh, Richard...*

(Violin music from an orchestra conveniently situated somewhere in a corner of the restaurant, eyes gazing, hands meeting across the table...)

'Jo? Do I look all right, d'you think? Or should I wear the suit after all?'

Jo surfaced from her film-directing dream and looked Mum up and down, then nodded. 'You look great, Mum.'

She didn't have to exaggerate; Mum really didn't look bad at all. She had on the jumper and a long black skirt, high-heeled shoes, a purply scarf and more make-up than usual. She knew Mum was trying to impress the teachers – for some reason Mum always felt intimidated by them – but Dad was bound to think it was all for his benefit. So far, so good...

The interview itself was over quickly. Jo had known it would be, as she had very definite ideas about what she wanted to choose – History, PE and German. Within half an hour of meeting Dad they were all back in the school foyer, being beamed at by Mrs Briand, one of the Deputy Heads. We must look like a happy family, Jo thought; well, last time they'd all come together for a parents' evening, they *had* been. As far as Jo knew. Perhaps she hadn't been able to see the cracks, that far back. She looked at Mum and Dad, momentarily seeing what Mrs Briand must see: an attractive married couple with their daughter. They looked right together, Mum and Dad. Still.

'Right, then.' Dad sounded brisk. 'Well, that was straightforward enough.'

'It's quite early,' Jo pointed out. 'I'm hungry, are you, Mum?'

'Yes, quite,' Mum said. 'There's a l—'

Jo, seeing the words 'lasagne in the fridge' forming on Mum's lips, jumped in quickly. 'Wouldn't you like to hear all about the Outdoor Pursuits week, Dad? We had a meeting about it yesterday. It sounds really great.'

This was where, according to Jo's script, Dad was supposed to come out with: 'I know! Let's go down to the Haycart. We can chat about it over a meal.'

But Dad didn't know his lines. He looked at his watch and said, 'You can tell me about it on Sunday week, can't you? I'd like to hear about it, yes. But I'm in a bit of a hurry. I've arranged to meet H—'

Time seemed to slow down and stop. The name 'Helen' was suspended in the air. Jo could sense Mum watching him intently, then Dad's mouth changed shape as if he'd decided to say 'someone' instead, and then he started again, with an air of having decided to go through with a difficult task. 'I've arranged to meet Helen at eight,' he said firmly, gazing at a display of Year Seven pastel drawings near the door as if they offered moral support.

Mum seemed to wilt a little, then stiffen. 'How fortunate,' she said frostily, 'that the meeting was over so quickly. You wouldn't want to be late. Come on then, Jo. Let's go and get ourselves something to eat. Thank you for coming,' she said to Richard, as if he were someone she'd only just been introduced to.

This wasn't how it was supposed to be! Mum was already on her way out of the door, smiling graciously at Mrs Briand who was now greeting Natalie and her parents and didn't notice. Mum spoiled her exit slightly by crashing into the display board and making it sway perilously. Jo glared at Dad. Why did he have to see Helen tonight? Couldn't he at least have spared the whole evening to sort out Jo's future? Wasn't she important enough? If she'd known, Jo would have spent an entire hour wavering between Art, Geography, Technical Drawing, Spanish and Goldfish Management – anything to spoil Dad's plans and keep Helen waiting. She had nothing against Helen personally, but this was *family*. Dad shouldn't squeeze in a quick meeting between social arrangements.

'Bye then, Dad,' Jo said grudgingly.

'Bye, Jo. I'll see you on Sunday week,' Dad said.

He kissed her, and she turned her cheek away just enough to let him know he was out of favour. He had spoiled all her plans and he didn't even know, let alone care. Jo hurried after Mum, half-expecting to see her dabbing at her eyes with a tissue. But Mum wasn't. She was talking to Judith's mum, jingling her car keys and looking quite cheerful.

'If you like, we could have a meal out somewhere,' Mum said brightly as they walked back to the car. 'I think we could treat ourselves, just for once. The Haycart's got midweek special offers and it's on our way home.'

Typical! Someone had been at her script, rewriting it, turning it into a situation comedy. Jo could picture what would happen next. She and Mum would sit down at a table and then Dad would walk in with Helen. Anyway, Mum couldn't afford to eat out. She was just trying to get one up on Dad.

'Oh, I'm not really all that hungry,' Jo mumbled. 'Beans on toast will do.'

Nathan

'It's the way she *doesn't* ask about Helen,' Jo told Lynette at registration next day. 'That's how I know she minds.'

Lynette was rummaging through her bag. 'I know I put it in here last night. Mrs Drake'll *kill* me if I don't hand it in today.'

'It's here.' Jo picked up the French exercise book from the desk and slapped it against Lynette's head. 'I mean, wouldn't you think she'd want to know *something*?' she continued. '"*What's she like, this Helen?*" or "*Is she pretty?*" Or even ask me whether I like her? I mean, wouldn't *you* want to know, if it was you?'

'Perhaps she thinks *you* mind. If you haven't said a word, she probably thinks you're avoiding the subject. Have you got a test in French today? We're having one, on all this vocabulary I haven't learned yet.'

Jo shook her head, to both remarks. 'No. Mum

minds all right. I could tell. The way she went all frosty and polite with Dad.'

She knew that bright, brittle smile, that air of cheerfulness that had just too much determination about it. It had been a complete wash-out, last night; Mum had played her part all right, but Dad had muffed his lines in a big way. Result: a distinct cooling of the atmosphere, several degrees' worth, nothing like the candlelit warmth Jo had hoped for.

'What's needed now is a different tactic,' she told Lynette. 'Get to work on Dad.'

Lynette looked sceptical. 'But *how?* Why do you think you're the one who's got to sort it out? It was them who decided to split up, after all. And they *are* grown-ups. They ought to know what they're doing.'

Jo huffed. 'They *think* they're grown-ups. Pity they don't behave like it. Honestly, I'm the only mature and sensible person in our—'

She almost said 'our family'.

'I don't think you ought to interfere,' Lynette persisted. 'Give your dad time. If it's just an infatuation thing with Helen – you know, it makes him feel good to have a younger girlfriend – you'll have to give him time for it to wear off.' Lynette looked across the form room, frowning. 'What's up with Amanda, d'you know?'

Jo looked. Amanda was sitting where she usually

sat, next to Ellie. Those two had been best friends for years, but now Amanda was turned away from Ellie, elbow resting on the table, hand propping her cheek to form a barrier. She was apparently engrossed in her homework diary, not normally a source of great fascination, but Jo could see the downturn of her mouth, and her face pink and puffy as if she'd been crying. Jo raised her eyebrows at Ellie, who pulled a wry face back and made a small don't-ask-me gesture. At the end of registration, Amanda got up without a word to Ellie and went out of the form room, rubbing a wrist across her eyes. Behind her, Jo heard Natalie Bayliss saying to Hayley, 'Can't take a joke, that's her trouble. What a cry-baby.'

Outside lessons, Natalie usually went around with Darren or a group of girls from the year above; she only consorted with Year Nine when there was no one else available. Her only friend in the form group was Hayley Jones, who like Natalie looked old enough to pass for Year Eleven. Both liked to amuse themselves by being nasty to other people, and Jo wondered what they'd said to Amanda. They seemed to pick on Amanda in particular, because for a while last term, when Natalie had been new and was finding her way around, Amanda had been friendly with her. It had been Ellie who had been upset then, Jo remembered – the odd one out in an oddly-assorted threesome. Then there had been all that business with Natalie and Mr Wishart, the History teacher who had left; Natalie had been in trouble for that, and although it wasn't their fault she had never forgiven Amanda or Ellie. In Jo's opinion, Natalie was a spiteful girl, best avoided; not the sort to forget a grudge or to make an effort to get on with others, and clever enough to make life unpleasant for anyone she disliked.

'What's wrong with Amanda?' Jo asked Ellie at the beginning of the lesson after break; they were both in Ms Aronson's set for French and usually sat next to each other. 'Is it Natalie, or what?'

Ellie nodded, looking round quickly at Natalie's empty place; Natalie was always last to arrive for lessons, taking the opportunity to linger between classrooms or spend ten minutes in the loo. 'Natalie started on at her on the way to school this morning, her and Hayley All-mouth. About how it's lucky Amanda's not going to Penhowell, because they wouldn't have ropes strong enough to hold her and she'd have to ride a carthorse instead of a pony. You know how touchy Amanda is about her weight. Now she's convinced herself that everyone'll be laughing about her when we get there. I keep trying to tell her not to take any notice, but she can't help it.'

'It's not as if Amanda's fifteen stone,' Jo said. 'I

mean, you wouldn't call her slim, but you wouldn't call her fat either. Unless you're Natalie. And who cares what Natalie thinks? Well, obviously,' she conceded, 'Amanda does. But she shouldn't.'

'You try convincing Amanda she's not fat,' Ellie said. 'She's one of those people who looks in the mirror and imagines she sees this disgusting flabby blob looking back. She hates being teased about it. She really does. And Natalie knows that.'

'Natalie would. She's like a vulture scenting blood.'

'I keep telling Amanda,' Ellie said feelingly, 'that if only she could pretend *not* to mind, if she could laugh and pretend it was a joke, Natalie would soon stop doing it. But it's not really as easy as that.'

'I know. There's no real way to get back at Natalie and make her shut up. If only you could call her Spotty or Big Nose or something, but there's nothing like that about her. It's not fair—'

Ellie made shushing gestures, and Natalie walked into the room – long-striding slim legs in black tights, shortest possible flared skirt, blonde hair falling over one eye – having managed, presumably, to tear herself away from Darren's enthusiastic clutches.

Ms Aronson looked up from her register. 'Where've you been, Natalie?'

'I had to see Mrs Reynolds about something,' Natalie lied smoothly.

'OK.' If Ms Aronson was in an officious frame of mind, she would check with Mrs Reynolds later, but today she looked keen to get on with the lesson. Natalie went to her place, only a slight smirk indicating that she'd got away with it. Again. The stale smell of cigarette smoke drifted from her clothes as she passed Jo's desk.

Only now did Jo notice that she'd got her History book on the desk in front of her instead of her French one. She bent to rummage in her rucksack. They were both red exercise books, and she must have picked up the wrong one from the kitchen table last night. Having got Lynette out of her panic, she was now faced with one of her own. Ms Aronson might put up with people arriving a few minutes late, but one thing that unfailingly brought out the full, devastating range of her sarcasm was when people didn't hand in their homework on time.

Today wasn't going smoothly. Jo spent most of lunchtime in Ms Aronson's room, redoing the French homework she'd already done last night, while Natalie, who Jo had seen copying hers from Sanjay before registration, went off to have another fag in the shrubby area behind the library where duty teachers usually forgot to look. In English, last lesson, Mr Barrington said he was fed up with preparing for their SATs, and he imagined everyone else was, too. Today they were going to do something different. He wanted them to get into pairs and interview each other.

'*Not* someone you already know, and certainly not your best friend,' he told them. 'I'm going to swap a few people around. Sanjay, you change places with Amanda; Jason, you swap with Greg; Eduardo, move up into that spare place; Jo, come and sit here; Damien, change with Natalie...'

After all this place-changing, Jo found herself partnered with Greg Batt. That was OK; Greg was a quiet, serious boy, who would answer her questions properly and not muck about, and would probably have some interesting ones to ask her. Mr Barrington had explained to them that the whole point of this was to ask open-ended questions (like "*How would you like to see yourself in ten years' time?*") rather than closed ones (like "*What size shoes do you take?*") so that you really found out about the person you were talking to. What they were like, what their ambitions were, their hopes and fears, not just how tall they were and what their favourite colour was. The idea, he said, was that they were pretending to be journalists, interviewing someone so that you could write a piece that gave a clear idea of their personality.

'Right then,' he called out, when everyone was

settled. 'Is anyone still sitting next to someone they know pretty well? If so, you'll have to move again. All right, Jason, you swap one more time – with Jo. Does that do it?'

Jo lugged her rucksack, book and pencil case to her new place, in the back row next to Nathan Fuller. He gave her a hostile look. She opened her draft book and anxiously read through the interview questions she'd written down, hastily scrawling out, *Do you get on well with your family?* Honestly, Mr Barrington could have *warned* them they were going to swap partners. There were some things you just couldn't ask Nathan. In fact, Jo wasn't sure what she *could* ask him that wasn't going to cause major offence. She looked around the classroom. At least Mr Barrington hadn't managed to pair up Natalie with Amanda.

'Do you want to start asking me first?' Jo suggested.

Nathan pushed his fringe out of his eyes and made a grunting noise which could have meant yes or no. Jo could see that he'd hardly written anything at all in his book, just a few notes with a lot of jagged crossing-out. He wasn't interested in finding out about her anyway. She was quite interested in finding out about him, but didn't see how she was going to do it in a way that would get any response.

'OK then, I'll start.' She did a bit more surreptitious

editing. 'What's your favourite sport?'

His brown eyes looked at her sharply, warily. 'That's a closed question. The sort you're not supposed to ask. I can just say "football", and that's all the answer you're going to get. Doesn't tell you much.'

He wasn't stupid, Nathan. He had been listening, and taking it in, even if he wasn't going to co-operate.

'All right, then. Why do you like football?'

''Cos I'm good at it.'

'Do you support a team?'

'Man United.' Nathan was staring at the desk, tilting his chair back and swinging his legs. Jo decided that her tactful approach wasn't getting her far, and picked one of her original questions. 'How do you see yourself in ten years' time?' she asked.

'Dead,' Nathan said, picking savagely at the broken edge of a thumbnail.

Well. That was a bit of a conversation-stopper. But Mr Barrington had told them that sometimes they'd need to ask extra questions, to find out more.

'Why dead?'

'No point staying alive,' Nathan said off-handedly.

Jo gazed at her draft book for inspiration. She was beginning to feel more like a Samaritan than a journalist, but a Samaritan without any idea what to say next. Was Nathan serious about wanting to be dead? Or was he saying it to be different, even just to be awkward?

'What don't you like about your life?' Jo said carefully. She could see Mr Barrington glancing in her direction from time to time. He knew what a difficult job he'd given her.

'Everything,' Nathan said. He looked at her defiantly and then added, ''Cept my dog.'

'Oh, have you got a dog?' Jo pounced on the idea – this was safer ground. She could talk about dogs. 'What's it like?'

'Not it. He. He's a Labrador. Black. Glossy. Mine.'

Nathan was still staring at the book in front of him but his expression had softened, his mouth curving in an almost-smile.

'Where did you get him?' Jo asked.

Nathan picked at his thumbnail, flicked a bit of dead skin across the desk and then said, 'Found him.'

'Was he abandoned, then? Someone threw him out?'

'Yeah. He was thin and scrawny, all bones. The only person he'd let touch him was me. He's OK now. I've trained him.'

'By yourself? You must be good with animals.'

'Yeah. I am.' Nathan said it matter-of-factly.

'What's his name?'

A pause, then Nathan raised his head and looked at Jo directly for the first time. 'He's called Gaz,' he said. He almost seemed to expect her to argue about it.

'That's an unusual name for a dog.'

'So what? That's his name. My dad chose it.'

'Oh.' This threw Jo, leaving her unsure what to ask next. 'Does Gaz live at your dad's house, then?' she asked cautiously.

Definitely the wrong thing to ask. Abruptly, Nathan's chair tipped upright, its front legs banging on the floor. His fingers started tearing at the pages of his draft book, scrabbling and ripping as if he wanted to hurt it.

'Nathan, don't—'

His face was brooding, shut in, angry. Jo had seen him look like that before. Usually, just before an explosion. She tried to think of something to say to calm him down.

'Never mind about your dad. Let's talk about Gaz.'

But it was too late for Nathan to be pacified. 'I'm not doing this any more,' he muttered. 'Stupid.' He picked up his exercise book and with a flick of his wrist send it flying, frisbee-style. Pages fluttering, it soared flatly across the room to hit Jason on the back of the neck.

'Oi! Who slung that?' Jason shouted, leaping up.

Nathan was out of his seat too, kicking it over,

barging past Jo, stumbling between the rows of desks with his face set and angry. Everyone looked round, all the interviews broken off, and then at Mr Barrington to see what he was going to do. He didn't shout or run after Nathan. He just walked calmly to Jo's desk and said to her, 'Go after him, could you? You seemed to be doing well just now.'

Yes, well – that was before I put my big foot in it, she thought. She left the classroom reluctantly, curious eyes watching her as she went. She was unsure where Nathan might have gone. Where *did* he go, when he stomped out of classrooms? He did it fairly often. Home, perhaps. But home wasn't really home to Nathan – he wanted to be with his dad. Jo didn't know where his dad lived, but she knew it was too far to run to.

She paused in the corridor. Being out of the classroom during lesson-time, even with permission, made her feel furtive, like the sort of person who went round plundering other people's bags and coat pockets. She imagined the fiercer of the two Deputy Heads coming round the corner and sweeping her off to the Year Head's office. While she stood dithering, quick footsteps came down the steps from the higher-level corridor at the office end, already too close for Jo to run away or hide. It was Mrs Reynolds, on her way to Mr Barrington's classroom.

'Why are you out of your lesson?' she asked Jo, not unpleasantly.

'Mr Barrington sent me after Nathan. To talk to him.'

Mrs Reynolds didn't seem surprised. She nodded and said, 'Righto. He's in my office.'

There had barely been time for her to catch Nathan behind the bike sheds or to waylay him as he bolted for the gate, so Jo could only assume he'd gone to her of his own accord. She went up the steps and cautiously opened the door. Nathan was there, sitting on a chair wedged into a space between a filing cabinet and a box of books. He looked at Jo guardedly, like a cornered dog that might be frightened into biting.

'Oh, hi,' Jo said. 'Mr Barrington sent me out after you.'

'Piss off,' Nathan spat at her. 'I'm not coming back.'

'No, I know. You don't have to.'

'It's stupid, what that bloke makes us do. I don't see what that's got to do with English.'

Jo sat down on Mrs Reynolds' chair. What now? She could hardly carry on nattering about Nathan's dog as if nothing had happened to interrupt their conversation. He watched her sit down, without comment. Jo decided to launch on the only relevant topic she could think of.

'My dad's left, too. Did you know? My mum and I are on our own. Well, with my nan.'

Nathan looked at her from under his fringe. His face was tight, a bit puffy, as if tears were only just held in check. Jo guessed that if he cried in front of her he'd be even more resentful. Ashamed. In the quietness of the office she was aware of his barely-contained aggression, aggression that could make him lash out unexpectedly or else turn inward to hurt himself. She was almost frightened of him, of the violent energy that coursed through him. He was like a letter-bomb sitting in the office, a parcel that might explode if handled carelessly. Perhaps that was his problem. His parents – his dad – treated him like a parcel, to be passed from one to the other, as it suited them.

''S not the same,' he said, in a voice so low that Jo could barely hear.

'No, I don't suppose it is. All families are different, aren't they? But my mum and dad split up and now they're getting divorced.'

'Your dad bought you that mountain bike,' Nathan said belligerently. 'I've seen it.'

'Yes, so that I can ride to school, now that Mum and I live so far away. I spend one week a month with my dad and the rest of the time with Mum.'

'That's more than I see my dad,' Nathan said. He

sniffed, and wiped a hand across his nose.

A girl would have asked for a tissue. Jo could see a box on Mrs Reynolds' desk, but she hesitated to offer one to Nathan. Absently, he wiped his hand on his sweater, and then started pulling at an unravelling hole in his sleeve, making it bigger.

'Did they fight, then, your mum and dad?' he said, throwing her a challenge. 'Mine did. All the time. Till she threw him out. Now she won't even say his name. She hates him.'

Physical fighting, hitting, pushing, or fighting with words, cutting the air with the savage thrusts and swipes that could hurt just as much? Jo didn't want to ask. She thought of home, her old home, made into a strange hostile place by the tension crackling in the air like electricity. Herself trying not to take sides, trying not to ask, trying to pretend nothing was wrong.

'Yes, they did,' she said. 'Perhaps it's best that they've split up – your parents I mean, *and* mine – if they can't stop fighting.'

What was she saying? After all her scheming and hoping to get her parents together? Was it really as hopeless as it obviously was for Nathan's parents?

Dogs were easier. Talk about dogs.

'I wish I could have a dog,' she said. 'I love dogs, but we can't have one in our small flat. I'd love to have a Labrador like your Gaz.'

'My mum hates dogs,' Nathan said fiercely. 'Says they're dirty. Only 'cos she can't be bothered.'

'Oh, I see,' Jo said sympathetically. 'So you can't have Gaz at home with you?'

Brisk footsteps, and Mrs Reynolds was back. 'OK, Jo, you'd better get back to your English lesson. Now then, young Nathan, what's going on?'

Typical!

'Bring in a photo of Gaz, if you've got one,' Jo said to Nathan. Outside the closed door, she pulled a face at Mrs Reynolds' name-plate. Just like adults to ask you to do something impossible, and then just when you were beginning to succeed, to barge in and take over. There was no point going back to English anyway now, since she'd got no partner. Though she'd found out quite a lot about Nathan, one way and another.

Ghost Shop

'That was unreasonable, if you ask me,' Lynette complained as they left the English room. 'Expecting you to go after weirdo Nathan. As if you could be expected to do anything when he's in that mood. Most of the teachers can't.'

'He's not that weird, really.' Jo felt obliged to stand up for Nathan. 'I mean, it's not his fault.' Ahead, people were spilling out of the corridor into the cold drizzle of a March afternoon. Jo pulled on her coat and zipped it up to her chin, anticipating an uncomfortable ride home.

'What did you do?' Lynette persisted. 'Hold his hand? Lie him down on a psychiatrist's couch?'

'No. Just talked a bit. Till Mrs Reynolds came barging in and told me to clear off.'

'So what did he say?'

They paused in the shelter of the overhanging upper floor, about to part: Jo heading for the main gate, Lynette for the primary school to collect her brothers.

'Well, it's confidential, isn't it?' Jo said doubtfully.

Lynette's eyebrows zoomed up into her hair. 'Oh, I see. You had quite a cosy chat, then? I didn't realise you got on so well.'

'We have got something in common, haven't we?' Jo said.

'Oh. Well, yeah. I s'pose.' Lynette looked embarrassed. 'Sorry. Is Nathan going to Penhowell next week?'

'Yes.' Jo stretched out a hand to see if it were really raining or just drizzling.

'They're letting him go? What if he throws a fit halfway up some mountain?'

'I don't suppose he will,' Jo said. She squinted up at the sky. 'I hope the weather won't be like this.'

Lynette giggled. 'My Mum's already taken over my packing. I keep telling her there's a whole week to go yet, but she won't listen. She's got this huge list on the side of the fridge and every time she's cooking she keeps remembering more and more things and dashing over to write them on. Clothes for wet weather, clothes for Arctic expeditions, clothes for a heat-wave. I'm going to need a separate coach all to myself if she goes on like this.'

'See you Sunday, then. It's too cold to stand about.'

Jo collected her bike and cycled off along wet shiny roads. Beyond the edges of town, the fields rose lush and damp on either side, beyond hedges shaded with the tiny green flames of emerging leaves. The ditches were splashed with celandines and violets. The mountain bike soared up the hill up to Farthingfield; really, Mum's old rattletrap would have been better for fitness purposes, but Jo hadn't ridden it for weeks now. Only another week of school, and then Wales – real mountains, rivers in spate, wild moorland. Jo felt herself tensing with excitement, longing for the remaining days to pass quickly.

Nan, coming in early from work, was in a similarly optimistic mood. She went into her room, turned on Radio 2 and started singing along tunelessly, banging about in her wardrobe and drawers. She was going away too – for her walking week in Norfolk. When she had finished packing, she emerged from her room to make herself an enormous packed lunch; then she polished up her boots to a high gloss and threaded them with brand-new peacock-blue laces.

'How are you getting there?' Jo asked, from the slipstream of all this activity.

'Dennis is picking me up at six,' Nan said. 'I'll be back on Friday, so if you want to borrow any of my outdoor gear, you can.'

'Thanks.' Jo couldn't quite see herself in Day-Glo

turquoise, but it was nice of Nan to offer.

This time, Jo was actually allowed a glimpse of Dennis when he came up to fetch Nan's bag. He was a big friendly man with grey hair and a tanned, creased skin and amazingly blue eyes. The clothes he wore, a lumberjack shirt and grey outdoor trousers with zipped pockets and reinforced knees, made him look ready to scale the nearest mountain. A pity there weren't going to be any mountains in Norfolk.

'You're off to the Brecon Beacons, I hear?' he said to Jo. 'Beautiful place. Pen y Fan and Corn Du – wonderful names, aren't they? Wish I was coming myself.' He smiled, revealing very white teeth.

'He seems nice, don't you think?' Jo remarked to Mum, when Nan and Dennis had said their goodbyes and left. 'Old, but young, if you know what I mean.'

'I'm glad you've managed to get over your prejudice of anyone over thirty,' Mum muttered, immersed in her accounts book.

Jo ate a biscuit, thoughtfully. 'The only thing is, if he likes real mountain walking in places like the Brecon Beacons, why does he go on silly little Ramblers' walks with Nan? You know the sort of thing. Taking ages to get over stiles. Having picnics every five minutes. Fussing if you get mud on your latest bit of Gore-tex. It's not the same sort of thing at all.'

'Mmm,' said Mum, sucking the end of her pen.

'Isn't there any dinner yet?' Jo looked round at the vacant cooker rings and at the saucepans all hanging in their places. 'I'm starving. What're we having?'

'Mmm?' Mum looked up, vaguely. 'Oh – there's a cold aduki bean pie in the fridge. We'll have it with salad. You can do oven chips if you like.'

'Cold aduki bean pie. Great,' Jo said, with heavy sarcasm that passed Mum by entirely. She opened the fridge door and looked at the pie sitting squidgily and unappetisingly under its cling-film. Oven chips? Mum didn't usually allow them in the house; she liked everything fresh. Proper food, not packaged stuff. However, Jo opened the freezer and there they were. She cut the packet open and spread some on a tray.

'I might as well put the pie in the oven too,' she said to Mum's bent head.

'Mmm. Whatever you like.'

Jo set the table, clattering the knives and forks reproachfully. Mum continued to stare at her page of accounts, oblivious.

'I've decided to drop History from my Options and do Hang-Gliding instead,' Jo announced.

'Mmm.'

'Mum!' Jo plonked the pepper-grinder down in front of her. 'You haven't been listening! What's the matter? Won't your accounts add up?'

Mum dropped her pen, letting it clatter on the table and then fall to the floor. She didn't pick it up. She looked at Jo with anxious, shiny eyes, her face tight.

'What's the matter?' Jo asked again. She picked up the pen and handed it back.

'The matter,' Mum said miserably, 'is that no, my accounts don't add up. And it's not my maths that's the problem. They don't add up because I can't get the shop to make money. No matter what I do.'

'Oh.' Jo's voice came out small and feeble.

'Takings are down again this week. Not by much, but still down. And even on a good week they aren't high enough. I can't pay off my loans, let alone make a profit. It's a failure, Jo.'

'Oh,' Jo said again, inadequately.

'*I'm* a failure,' Mum said, slamming the book shut. Both she and Jo stared at it. The slap of heavy pages lingered in the air.

'What are you going to do?' Jo asked.

'I don't know what I *can* do. I've tried working harder. Cooking more recipes, more variety. That's no good. I need to get more customers in, and there just aren't the people in the High Street any more. I stand at the shop door and look, and even on a Saturday there's hardly anyone around. People go down to Sainsbury's and the DIY shops in their cars and don't use the High Street shops. I'm in the wrong place.'

Jo remembered Nan's *ghost town* phrase. It was true. The town *was* a ghost town, and Mum's shop looked like turning into a ghost shop. A shop haunted by Mum and a few spectral figures searching the shelves for tofu burgers and almond slices. It wasn't fair! Mum put so much effort into that shop, so much *love* into cooking her special dishes, all wholesome and herby and spicy and delicious (well, apart from the aduki bean pie). People didn't know what was good for them. They were all down at the new precinct eating Death Burgers and chips and ice-cream, when they'd have been far better off in Mum's shop buying fennel patties and halva and helping Mum to keep going. Didn't they *care*? Well, no, of course they didn't. Why should they?

'Can't you move down next to Sainsbury's?' Jo suggested.

'Of course I can't,' Mum huffed. 'There aren't any small shop units down there, and even if there were, I wouldn't be able to afford one. I only got this shop because it was so cheap. I suppose no one else was idiotic enough to take it on. You only have to look at the number of other small shops going out of business.' She propped her head in both hands. 'There's only one way to improve things, and that's to put more money into it. Expand. Be more dynamic.

Go in for catering, or run a café. But that would mean buying all sorts of new equipment, employing staff to do the cooking and wait at tables, and it still wouldn't bring more people into the High Street. Anyway, I haven't got more money to put in. I'm stretched to the limit as things are.'

Jo could think of only one solution. 'Couldn't you ask Dad for some money?'

'*No!*' Mum glared at her. 'I'm not asking him for help! And that's definite. He thought I was stupid in the first place, to try. He was right.' She sounded hopeless. 'He's got far more business sense than I have. Perhaps I should have listened.'

'But then you'd still be working in some dreary old office.'

'Perhaps I will anyway. If I really have to give up.'

Wildly, Jo pictured the three of them homeless, begging for food in the High Street or sleeping in cardboard boxes down by the lorry park. What would happen to them, if Mum had to give up the shop? Where would they get money from? Jo swiftly told herself not to be ridiculous. Nan must have a stash of money somewhere – she'd helped with the shop, but perhaps there was still some left over from the sale of her bungalow – she wouldn't stand by and watch the shop flounder. Jo clung to that idea like a lifebelt, to stop herself being swept away with the depression that was pulling Mum down. Anyway, she thought, someone had to stay sane and practical, the mood Mum was in. Mum needed common-sense advice, not hysteria. But Jo couldn't think of any practical solution, since her mother was so adamant about not asking Dad for help. The problem was like a maze – when you turned a corner to find your way out, a new barrier presented itself.

'Surely there must be *something* we can do! You're not seriously giving up?'

'I don't know. I don't know.' Mum buried her face in her hands.

Jo looked around the cluttered kitchen at Mum's jars of ingredients, herbs and spices, stacks of cake tins. More was at stake than just giving up the shop, she realised. If Mum had to admit defeat, it would be admitting to the failure of her independence.

'Can't I help out more, in the shop?' Jo said.

Mum uncovered enough of her face to reveal a small, tired smile. 'Thanks, Jo. I know you want to help. But you do your bit already, and I don't want to take up more of your time, not with your exam years coming up soon. It's not fair to make you feel tied to the shop. No, I need to make big changes or else give up. I've been pretending for long enough. I'll have to face facts.'

Jo's glance fell on a heap of books at one end of the table: Mum's latest Frankenstein Club reading. She had moved on to the Victorians: *Jane Eyre*, *The Tenant of Wildfell Hall* and *Wuthering Heights* were stacked there, together with a slim pamphlet called *The Brontës at Haworth*. The Brontës had been sitting on the table untouched for the last week, as far as Jo was aware. Mum had begun her course with such enthusiasm and now the problems with the shop looked like spoiling that, too.

Jo made up her mind. If Mum wouldn't ask Dad for help, she would ask him herself. Dad could always send the money in secret or something. He could be a mysterious benefactor, as in that bit from *Great Expectations* Mr Barrington had read to the class once. But no, that wouldn't work – Mum would have to *know* who had saved the shop, so that she could be properly grateful.

'Come on, Mum. Let me make you a cup of tea,' Jo said, suddenly cheerful. 'It'll work out. You'll see.'

Mum fished a tissue out of her sleeve and blew her nose. 'Thanks, love. I'm sorry to be so droopy. It's not fair to worry you about it.'

'Oh, that's all right,' Jo said. She had to make an effort not to sound positively happy, now that the idea had presented itself to her. Dad wouldn't want to see the shop all empty and boarded up, or Mum on the council housing list. He'd offer to do something to help, Jo was certain. She began working out how she would tell him.

Jo: (casually) *Dad, you know how hard Mum works in the shop?*

Dad: (trying not to sound too interested) *Yes?*

Jo: *Well, it would be an awful pity if all that hard work came to nothing, wouldn't it?*

Dad: *What do you mean, nothing? Why should it?*

Jo: (telling him straight) *Dad, Mum needs your help.*

Dad: (trying not to sound too eager, or to say 'I told her so' – pretending to sound surprised) *Oh? What sort of help…?*

Jo chose Mum's favourite mug from the row of hooks, the one with purple irises on it. This brilliant new idea could be just what was needed to get Mum and Dad back together again – Dad would feel flattered to be asked for help, Mum so keen to smother him in gratitude that she'd forget all their previous rows; Helen would quietly and obligingly take her cue to *exit, stage left*, as if she'd never been on the cast list at all.

Dad had better learn his lines properly this time.

Penhowell

'So when are you going to ask him, then?' Lynette asked.

Jo was sitting on top of the stairs, cradling the telephone and keeping a careful ear open for Mum getting out of her bath. 'I can't, now. That's the point. I had it all planned out, what I was going to say to him. Now I won't get the chance. Dad's just phoned to say he's going on some boring old business management course all next week so could I put off my week there till I come back from Wales. I'm going to have to wait a whole fortnight.'

'Still,' Lynette pointed out, 'if he's doing business management, he'll learn all sorts of useful stuff for your mum.'

Jo considered this. 'I s'pose so.' She had the cynical idea that Dad's business course was more to do with making massive sums of money for *Toyz World* and forcing all its rivals out of business, but maybe

Lynette had a point. 'Anyway, so I won't be coming over tomorrow afternoon, now I'm not going to Dad's.' She and Lynette had planned to go for a final pre-Wales run, a longer one than usual.

'Oh. So we can't do our run.' Lynette's voice expressed a mixture of disappointment and relief. 'Can't you bike over anyway, just for the afternoon?'

'I could come over on Sunday if you like, but tomorrow Mum wants us to go out somewhere. To make up for Dad, I suppose. She says it's ages since we had a day out together, and I suppose it is – she's always working or too tired. She's actually *closing the shop*, that's how fed up with it she is.'

On Saturday, Jo and Mum got up early and caught the bus to Oxford. Mum said it was a pity to live within reach of a place like Oxford but never to spend a day there, and besides she wanted to visit some good bookshops, her course having given her a taste for more intellectual reading than the local library could cater for.

It wasn't altogether a happy day. There was a sort of desperation about Mum's need for them to have a thoroughly good time. 'This is nice,' she kept saying, and 'Are you enjoying yourself?' and 'Do say if there's something you'd rather do, won't you?' Jo felt that she had to wear a permanent idiotic grin, to convince

Mum that she was having the best day ever. It was as if Mum wanted to prove something. She insisted on going to *The Oxford Story*, in spite of the expense, and then they took a sightseeing bus round the city, the sort of bus that had an open-top roof and a guide giving a commentary on all the buildings and colleges they passed. It was too cold for anyone else to brave the open top floor, but Mum wanted to do the whole tourist bit, so Jo had to keep admiring stone building and spires and wrought-iron gates giving glimpses of perfect lawns and swathes of daffodils, while trying not to let her teeth chatter.

Mum had brought a picnic lunch, because eating out in Oxford would be too expensive, so they found a park and sat by the river to eat. Then she wanted to go to Blackwells Bookshop. 'I'll need to spend a long time looking,' she told Jo, 'so why don't you go back to that outdoor shop we just passed and get yourself something for next week?' She handed Jo a ten-pound note.

'Thanks, Mum,' Jo said doubtfully. She knew Mum couldn't afford to fling ten-pound notes about, but she went back to the outdoor shop and looked at the rainbow displays of costly Gore-tex and fleece, and wondered what on earth she could buy that would please Mum. Eventually she bought a waterproof zip-up wallet, which left her five pounds change, and wandered back to find Mum. Mum was deep in the literary criticism section of Blackwells, and had bought herself just one paperback book, a biography of Charlotte Brontë.

They walked back through the busy streets to the bus station. The pavements were crowded with Saturday shoppers and it occurred to Jo that if only Mum could move her shop *here*, she might be able to make it work. But of course that was daft – Mum might just as well think of buying the whole of Harrods as consider renting a shop in Oxford. Mum had become quiet and thoughtful since they left Blackwells, and when they came across a health-food shop and Mum said, 'Oh, I must just have a quick look in here,' Jo knew that her thoughts were heading in the same direction.

'That was – a bad mistake,' Jo puffed, running alongside Lyn on Sunday afternoon. 'Everything in there – cost more than it does at Mum's – but people were – still buying it. There were about – fifteen people in there – all filling baskets – with all this expensive stuff – can't we slow down a bit? – I'm getting a stitch.'

'You shouldn't try to run and talk. It interferes with your breathing,' said Lynette, but slowed her pace a little.

'It's all right for you,' Jo panted, 'you've got longer legs.'

'And I don't talk as much,' Lynette said between carefully measured breaths.

'Anyway, the point is – now I feel really bad – about going – when she's so depressed—'

All Jo had been able to think of to suggest to Mum was, 'Maybe there are fifteen customers waiting outside our shop, this very minute.' Mum had laughed and said, 'No, these are the same fifteen people. They found my shop closed so they all got the bus down to Oxford instead, to stock up.' Jo could tell that, in spite of her flippant tone, she really was having doubts about closing the shop. This could have been the one day when everyone in Beckley decided to switch to a healthy diet.

'You'll have to go.' Lynette's feet pounded out the rhythm to her words. 'You can't back out now. Your Nan'll be back next week.'

'Big consolation that'll be,' Jo huffed.

Jo never seriously had any intention of not going, but all the same she felt awful on Friday morning, saying goodbye, reassuring Mum that she had enough thick socks and had remembered to put her toothbrush in at the last minute. Jo caught the bus today, because of her bag of stuff for the week. It felt odd going to school in her own clothes – boots, jeans and sweatshirt – instead of school uniform. The coach was leaving straight after lessons.

'What other teachers are going?' Amanda asked at registration, having got over her disappointment enough to take a slight interest.

'Steve, Mrs Hughes and Miss Kelland,' Jo said.

'Miss Kelland? But she's a History teacher!'

'They can't have *all* the PE staff out of school, all at once, can they?'

'All the same,' Amanda said, 'I can't see what use Miss Kelland is going to be.'

'She might be brilliant. How do you know she's not an Olympic canoeist or a mountain-climber in her spare time?'

'It'll be her last week, won't it?' Amanda said. 'She's leaving at the end of term. That means we'll get yet *another* History teacher next term.'

They had a History lesson later that morning. Miss Kelland had left off her usual short skirt in favour of tight jeans and a sweatshirt.

'Are you going on the Wales trip, Miss?' asked Eduardo, who wasn't, and someone else wolf-whistled.

Miss Kelland didn't reprimand the wolf-whistler, but only nodded and giggled, as if she quite liked being whistled at.

'Wish I was going, then,' said Eduardo. 'Who'll be taking us for History next week?'

'A supply teacher. And there's a new teacher starting next term.'

'Supply teacher? Great!' Eduardo turned round to his friends. 'If it's that daft old bat with glasses, we can do nothing all week. She's too soft to notice.'

'Don't worry. I've set you lots of important work to do.' Miss Kelland sat down, crossing her legs rather self-consciously.

'Oh, Miss! What, last week of term? If it's so important, how come the others aren't doing it?' Eduardo demanded.

'I expect they'll do it when they get back from Wales,' Miss Kelland said vaguely.

'Will we hell,' Natalie muttered behind Jo.

'She hasn't set us any work, anyway,' Hayley muttered back. 'What does she think we are, telepathic?'

'We've already got tons of Maths to do, from Mr O'Shaughnessy,' Natalie complained. 'Double homework, he called it. More like quadruple.'

Must be Murphy's Law, Jo thought. Natalie, Hayley and their friend Leanne from another form had all got places at Penhowell, whereas Amanda, along with several other people Jo would have preferred, hadn't.

There was a holiday atmosphere when they all finally piled on the coach at a quarter to four. It was as good as the end of term – it would be the Easter break as soon as they came back. There was plenty of room to spread themselves out on the coach, with three staff and only thirty pupils: nine from Jo's form, the rest from elsewhere in the year group, including some she didn't know by name. The coach headed west with the Friday traffic, leaving the motorway behind as the countryside became hillier and wilder. Jo felt excitement rising inside her with the contours – she could see remote farmhouses, winding tracks, purplish hills, dark clumps of woodland capped with misty cloud. Mr Kershaw switched on the loudspeaker to draw everyone's attention to the red dragon sign by the roadside which meant they were entering Wales, and from now on all the road signs were in Welsh as well as in English. Everyone started trying to twist their tongues into the strange words.

Narrow lanes replaced the main roads, and the coach often had to pull over against the hedge to let another car pass. It was dusk by the time the coach driver drew up, apparently in the middle of nowhere. Mr Kershaw got to his feet and faced the pupils.

'This is as close as we can get,' he explained. 'The track's too narrow for the coach to go up. Collect your bags from the hold, and then we'll go up to the Lodge.'

Outside, there was a board saying PENHOWELL OUTDOOR PURSUITS CENTRE, with the red dragon sign, and then an uphill cinder track leading between hedges. Waiting for the driver to unload the bags, Jo sniffed the air. Grass, earth, sheep dung, and a sort of mineraly water smell. They had passed through the nearest village about three miles back, and that was only a little cluster of cottages around a church. This was real country: damp, wild and remote.

'I don't see why the coach couldn't go all the way up to the house,' Hayley grumbled, as they started to lug their bags. 'My arms are killing me.'

'Come on, Hayley.' Mr Kershaw was always cheerful. 'You've only just started! How are you going to manage on the way up Pen y Fan?'

'Penny what?'

'Pen y Fan. The highest mountain in the Brecon Beacons. All 886 metres of it.'

'Are you winding me up?'

Mr Kershaw pretended to consider deeply. 'Well, perhaps I'm exaggerating a bit. It might be only 885.'

Hayley's pace slowed even further. 'Oh God. What have I let myself in for?'

Jo couldn't help giggling at the sight of two of the boys ahead, Scott Mayhew and Greg Batt, going up the track side by side. The difference in their height made them look a ridiculous pair – Greg had shot up recently and was nearly six foot, whereas Scott was still so small that he could have been mistaken for someone in primary school. Besides that, Scott had his luggage in a smart suitcase with little wheels attached, and he was trundling it along the bumpy track as if heading for an airport departure lounge.

The Lodge must have once belonged to a big country estate, but now it was rather dilapidated – a sprawling building of grey slate, with rush matting on the floors. Two instructors were there to meet the group, both young and friendly and dressed in scarlet sweatshirts. Steve Kershaw directed the group into what he called the meetings room, which was laid out like a classroom with rows of wooden seats and a whiteboard at the front. The instructors introduced themselves as Gary and Imogen, and then Mr Kershaw said he'd better get the bedrooms organised before anything else.

'OK,' he began, producing a list. 'The girls are in rooms of six each, and we've got eighteen girls, so that works out just right. The boys are on the top floor in two fives and a four. There's to be no arguing about who shares with who, all right? I've worked this out carefully and I need to know who's where. So does the Centre, for their fire regulations. So no swapping. Room One. Natalie Bayliss, Ellie Byrne, Jo Cannon, Lynette Colburn, Hayley Jones, Leanne Taylor. Off you go then, girls. Don't stand about looking gormless. Get your stuff and sort out who's having which bunk. Down here in ten minutes for dinner. Room Two—'

Jo went out of the room behind Ellie, who was looking positively sick.

'I can't share a room with Natalie and those other two, I just *can't*,' she told Jo in an anguished whisper.

Jo was equally appalled, but hoped she was hiding it better. She had expected that they'd be able to *choose* who they shared with, in which case she, Lynette and Ellie would have asked to be with Judith, and anybody else other than Natalie.

'Perhaps it won't be all that bad,' she said. 'There's three of them and three of us.'

'Can't we ask to change?'

'You heard what Steve said. No swapping.'

On the upstairs landing they drew level with Lynette, who pulled a face but said nothing. Natalie and the other two had already gone into the room to bag the beds they wanted. There were three pairs of bunks, which meant that someone would have to share one with Leanne. She didn't look too pleased at the prospect. The other three hesitated, until Jo, knowing that Ellie felt like the odd one out and would feel obliged to offer, said, 'I'll share with Leanne,' and dumped her bag on the bottom bunk. She would have preferred a top one, but this wasn't the time to be awkward. Ellie gave her a grateful smile and took the bottom bunk of the other pair.

It was a large, high–ceilinged bedroom with a fireplace, no longer used, flowered curtains at the windows, and bare board floors. There was a washbasin in one corner and a hanging rail for clothes, and a map of the Brecon Beacons pinned to the wall near Jo's bunk. Jo went to the window and looked out, but it was too dark to see more than pinpoints of light in the direction of the village.

'Coming down then, Nat? I'm starving,' Leanne said.

'Hang on a minute. I'm having a fag first.' Natalie was rummaging in her bag.

Jo and Lynette exchanged glances, and Jo said, 'In here? Are you joking? There are *No Smoking* notices downstairs and anyway you know what Steve said about smoking on school trips.'

'They'll smell the smoke. They're bound to come round the rooms,' Lynette pointed out.

Ellie glanced up at the ceiling. 'There's a smoke detector.'

'I'll open the window and lean out, dimmo. D'you

think I'm halfwitted?' Natalie said, lighting up. 'Want one, Hay?'

'No thanks. And hurry up.'

Jo flung both windows wide open. 'Go on then, lean out, if you *must* smoke. Don't blame us if you end up getting sent home.'

'Don't worry. You won't spoil your shining reputations,' Natalie said sarcastically, ambling towards the window. 'Why d'you think Steve put you in here with us? So you can check up on us. You can go straight down and tell him if you like.'

'I don't know why you have to light up two seconds after you get here,' Lynette said. 'You're only doing it to show off.'

'Oh, yeah?' Natalie sucked on her cigarette. 'Show off to who? Think I need to impress you three? Want a fag, Ellie? You never did quite get the hang of it, did you, that time in the park—'

Jo didn't know what Natalie meant by that, but Ellie turned bright red and became engrossed in examining one of the straps of her bag.

'Give it a rest, Nat,' Hayley said, unexpectedly. 'I'm going down even if you're not. I'm famished.'

Lynette glanced in the mirror above the washbasin and smoothed down her hair. 'Let's go,' she said to Jo and Ellie. 'We can unpack later.'

They went down to the entrance hall, finding no

one there, as the others were still in their rooms. Jo saw that Ellie was close to tears. Ellie wasn't normally a fusser; she was genuinely upset.

'Come on, Ellie,' she said. 'You can't let Natalie spoil this trip. We're going to have a fantastic week.'

Ellie shook her head. 'Not if I have to share with Natalie, I won't. If I ask Miss Kelland if I can change rooms, will you both say you want to as well?'

'I don't know,' Lynette said. 'Miss Kelland's only been here one term – she doesn't know what Natalie's like. She won't understand. And besides, won't that only make it worse? Wouldn't it be best to pretend we don't mind?'

'Remember what you said to Amanda the other day,' Jo said. 'Letting Natalie know she's getting to you is the best way to make her carry on. You mustn't take any notice.'

'But I can't take no notice,' Ellie said miserably. 'You heard Natalie just now. She'd be picking on Amanda if Amanda had come. Now she's going to pick on me. And do her best to get us all into trouble.'

'No, she won't,' Jo said. 'Not all three of us. Someone's got to share with those three, and Miss Kelland will say why shouldn't it be us. We'll have to put up with it.'

Trust

Although Jo was determined that sharing a room with Natalie wasn't going to spoil the week, she couldn't help feeling that Fate had been a little careless. First, by allowing Natalie's, Hayley's *and* Leanne's names to be pulled out of the hat, when there were far nicer names in there (and in any case those three had only wanted to come to get a week off school, as far as Jo could tell). Second, by letting Mr Kershaw think of cramming six such ill-assorted people into one room.

It was for Ellie's sake rather than her own that she decided to approach Mr Kershaw. The evening meal was over and he was having a cup of coffee with Miss Kelland before getting everyone together again.

'Look, I know you said there wasn't going to be any swapping of rooms,' she began tentatively, 'but it's not a very good idea to have Ellie in with Natalie. They don't get on at all.'

Mr Kershaw stirred his coffee and gave the faintest of sighs, as if he'd anticipated this sort of problem. 'Who would she rather be with, then?'

'Well, with Lynette and me, and perhaps Judith, or practically anyone else, really.'

'But she *is* in with you and Lynette.'

'Yes, I know, but Natalie's going to be nasty to her. She's started already.'

Mr Kershaw frowned. 'I don't see what I can do. It's not as if she's on her own with no friends at all. Are you asking me to move all *three* of you? Sorry – I'm not going to. Once I start giving in to you, I'll have ten other people moaning that they're not where they want to be.'

'Do you want me to have a word with Natalie?' Miss Kelland suggested.

'No, thank you,' Jo said quickly. No No NO! The last thing she wanted was for Natalie to know she'd been complaining to the teachers. You'd think Miss Kelland would know that, in spite of being new.

'I'll make sure Ellie and Natalie aren't put together for any of the team things,' Mr Kershaw conceded.

'Problem?' Gary, the instructor, came over with a cup of black coffee and sat down with the teachers. He smiled at Jo in a way that made her think there wouldn't be any serious problems while he was around.

'No, not really.' She didn't want Gary or Mr Kershaw to think she was the sort of person who whined and made difficulties all the time. She wasn't. She prided herself on being able to get on with things, being able to confront problems.

'Part of this week is being able to get on with other people, Jo,' Mr Kershaw said, echoing her thoughts. 'Working as a team. It doesn't matter whether you specially like the people you're with, or not. You can't let personal squabbles get to you when you're hanging by a rope.'

'No, I know,' Jo said. 'OK. Thanks. I'll tell Ellie.'

She left them to their coffee, annoyed by the fact that Gary's first impression of her would be as a whinger.

The rest of the evening went well. Gary and Imogen explained the rules of the Centre and made them do a fire drill, then outlined the activities for the week and organised a team quiz based on map skills. People were allowed to choose their own teams for this, and Jo's group – Jo, Lynette, Ellie and Greg Batt – won. They were each awarded a bar of Kendal Mint Cake as a prize.

'Survival rations,' Gary told them, handing over the wrapped bars. 'To be kept in your rucksacks, not eaten in your dorm tonight.'

Already, Gary was proving to be an unexpected

bonus as far as most of the girls were concerned: young and muscular, with short blond hair and clean-cut good looks. ('All right if you like Blue Peter presenters,' Natalie said, but Jo had seen her looking.) The other instructor, Imogen, was much quieter; apart from introducing herself she left it to Gary to organise the evening. She was small and very slim, and didn't look tough enough to scramble up rocks or manage a canoe.

Mr Kershaw had said that everyone was to be in their room by half past nine, in bed by ten and asleep by ten-thirty. Jo had a feeling that this wasn't going to be easy in her particular room, and was proved right when Natalie produced a radio and turned up the volume. Natalie and the other two seemed to have taken over, spreading their belongings everywhere (this room wasn't likely to win the week's prize for neatest dormitory), and they took a very long time getting ready for bed, wandering around half-undressed. Jo, Lynette and Ellie undressed primly in the shower room, and got straight into their bunks. Ellie tried to read a book, Lynette was already writing a postcard to the twins and Jo wanted to get to sleep early, eager for the day ahead. Climbing, abseiling and canoeing. Unfortunately, she suspected that for Natalie and the other three the daytime activities would take second place to night-time socialising. It was clear that Natalie had something else hidden in her bag beside the cigarettes – various hints had been dropped – but Jo wasn't going to show any interest.

'Isn't it about time you turned that radio off?' she burst out, having tried to muffle her ears in her pillow for some while.

'Past your bedtime?' Natalie said, with a patronising smile.

'Yes, it is. I've come here for the climbing and stuff, not to spend half the night talking.'

'Who was talking to you?' Leanne said.

At that point there was a rapping on the door, and a female voice said, 'Time to be quiet now, girls. You've got an early start in the morning.' Then the door opened and Miss Kelland came in, dressed in a red tartan dressing-gown. 'Turn the radio off now, Natalie. Come on. You heard what Mr Kershaw said.'

'OK,' Natalie said, in the bright girlish voice which she could put on when she wanted to deceive unwary teachers. 'Goodnight, Miss. Sleep well.'

'I'm turning the lights off. Everyone OK? 'Night, then.'

'I wonder where she's spending the night?' Natalie said, as soon as Miss Kelland had gone. 'With Steve Kershaw, I bet.'

'You reckon?' Leanne asked, impressed.

'She fancies him. It's obvious. Did you see them sitting together after dinner?'

'Where are their rooms?'

'Top floor,' Natalie said. 'Single rooms. I saw the plan on the notice board downstairs. Mrs Hughes is down here. Suspicious, or what?'

'That's rubbish, Natalie!' Jo couldn't help joining in. 'All the boys' rooms are up on the top floor. And anyway Steve's married, with a baby. He wouldn't do anything like that.'

'You're so naive it's not true,' Natalie said, arranging her pillow. 'You think married people don't have affairs? What about your dad? I've seen him out a couple of times with someone who's not your mum.'

'That's not the same,' Jo said angrily. 'He and my mum don't live together any more. That was Helen you saw – I've met her, it's no secret. It doesn't matter if Dad does have aff— if he *is* seeing someone else.'

'Well, it obviously matters to you,' Natalie said.

Jo had done exactly what she had advised Ellie against – let Natalie know that one of her digs had hit home. Not trusting herself to say any more, she turned her face resolutely to the wall, determined to sleep. It wasn't easy, but after about another hour of listening to conversations about every item of Miss Kelland's clothing and appearance, how hunky

Gary was, and what Natalie and Darren did together, where, when and how, the words and laughter finally drifted into the background and she slept.

Gary had explained all about abseiling back in the centre and had demonstrated the harness, karabiners and ropework. It was all perfectly safe, he kept emphasising, as long as you did what you were told. Although Jo felt quite sure he knew what he was doing, she couldn't stop her stomach from giving a huge lurch when they walked the short distance from the coach and stood at the base of the cliff they were going to abseil down. It towered ominously, the rock wet and shiny with rain. The face was craggy, with tiny plants and tufts of grass growing in defiance of the elements wherever they could get a roothold. The ledge at the top looked an immense distance away – the height of two houses at least. Jo began to regret the baked beans she had eaten at breakfast.

I'm not going to let myself down, she told herself. Ha! Letting yourself down was exactly what you did, abseiling. *OK, then, I'm not going to make a fool of myself.*

'We walk up an easy path to get to it. The climbing bit comes later,' Gary explained. 'I'm taking four people up, first, while the others watch from here. But everyone's going to do it. Who wants to start?'

Jo's hand went up as if of its own accord.

'Well done, Cannonball,' Steve Kershaw said. 'And let's have – er – Lynette, Sanjay and Craig.'

They were in a small group today, fifteen pupils and two adults, the others having gone pony-riding with Imogen and Mrs Hughes. Following Gary up a track which turned into a winding path between rocks, Jo wished she didn't feel like a broiler chicken on its way to be slaughtered. It was a cold spring day, the wind coming from the east and bringing with it a spattering of rain. The weather made Jo more tense than she would have felt on a still, sunny day. On both sides, the valley slopes rose high, in shades of green and purple, their summits obscured by shifting cloud. It was exactly the kind of scenery Jo had come for, but now her thoughts were dominated by the task ahead. She heard the baa-ing of sheep and the hoarse chacking of some mountain bird. This wasn't a proper mountain, only a craggy edge used by climbers for practising, but it felt high enough to Jo by the time she reached the ledge and looked down at the yellow helmets and upturned faces of those waiting below. She felt like someone waiting to do an Olympic high dive. Her stomach churned.

Gary was helping Steve Kershaw to get into the harness, checking the karabiner was properly attached to the front, fixing a belay to a crag of rock and giving a firm tug to show everyone how secure it was. Mr Kershaw had done this before and wasn't in the least nervous. He went right to the edge, so close that Jo felt sick, then turned round and leaned out from the ledge, his weight on the rope. Then he dropped out of sight. Jo closed her eyes; it would be her turn in a moment. When she opened them, Lynette was looking at her as if they were about to be parted for ever.

They heard Mr Kershaw making some joke from halfway down, and seconds later he was at the bottom, unfastening himself and waving to Gary as a signal to pull the harness back up.

Gary grinned at Jo. 'OK, then? Your turn. Helmet on straight?' He helped her into the sit-harness – a strong waist-belt and loops round the tops of her legs – adjusted the fastenings, and reminded her how to use her left and right hands to let the rope slip through the friction device, or to stop it. She looked down at his tanned hairy wrists and knew that she would do whatever she was told, rather than admit to being scared senseless. He had talked last night about trust and teamwork, and she understood now that she was about to do something that defied common sense – step backwards off a yawning drop – because the brief amount of training had given her trust.

She leaned back into cold, damp air, into

nothingness. The first few moments were the worst. Trying not to think about the drop below. Trying not to imagine what would happen if the ropes snapped. They wouldn't snap, Gary had demonstrated that. She felt the comforting pull against her waist and legs.

Gary smiled at her. 'OK, down you go. Not too fast.'

She remembered what she had been shown, and started to let the rope slip through the figure-eight, controlling the speed of her descent. A few seconds later, she felt like laughing aloud. It *was* easy – bouncing down the slope, feet skipping off the surface, letting the rope out more quickly as she gained in confidence. Too soon, the ground came tilting up at her from some odd angle and her feet struck down. Her head slowly got back to normal; it was like being on a roundabout and then coming to a sudden stop. She felt a sense of anticlimax – it had been great, but it was all over too soon. She wanted to do it again.

'Well done, Jo,' Miss Kelland encouraged. 'You made it look easy. I'll be terrified.'

Lynette came down more slowly than Jo, almost walking, looking anxiously over her shoulder the whole time. Then Sanjay, with war-whoops, and Craig, who looked terrified even after reaching the ground safely. Steve Kershaw walked up with the next group of four, which included Miss Kelland. The three pupils – Greg, Nathan and Judith – came down with no fuss, and then it was Miss Kelland's turn.

'She told me she's terrified of heights,' Lynette told Jo. 'Do you think she'll be able to do it?'

''Course she will. She's not going to let herself be shown up by a bunch of fourteen-year-olds, is she?'

All the same, there was a considerable delay at the top. Hayley walked back from the rock face a few metres for a better look.

'They're *both* helping her, Steve *and* Gary,' she announced. 'Looks like she's bottling out.'

Natalie giggled. 'Making the most of it, if you ask me. Two blokes all to herself.'

'It's not fair if teachers are allowed to bottle out,' Leanne complained. 'If she doesn't do it, then I'm not.'

'No, she's coming down. Look.'

Miss Kelland was lowering herself in jerky rushes, Steve Kershaw shouting encouragement from above. She reached the ground, flushed and breathless. Lynette went to help her disentangle herself from the harness.

'That was terrifying, at least until I got started,' Miss Kelland gasped, brushing damp strands of hair from her eyes. 'I'd never have done it without Ste—

without Mr Kershaw helping me.'

Jo thought of Natalie's remarks about Miss Kelland and Mr Kershaw. Outrageous as the suggestion was, there was something about the way Miss Kelland said his name. As if she liked saying it.

'Are you OK, Gina?' Mr Kershaw shouted down.

'Fine, thanks,' Miss Kelland shouted back. 'OK, Natalie, Hayley, Scott and Judith, you go next. I bet you do better than I did,' she added with a shaky grin.

Gina. Jo tried out the name. Gina and Steve. They went well together, as names. But she reminded herself that Steve was married, with a baby son – he had brought photos in to show the form group, as if the baby were a wonderful present he couldn't resist showing off to everyone. Surely *all* adults weren't busy having secret affairs and fancying each other and swapping partners? Surely Mr Kershaw wouldn't show off his baby son one minute and then have an affair with a pretty young teacher the next, all in full view of Year Nine? Jo felt that she would never understand adults. Why did they have to make life so difficult? And for some reason she felt particularly let down by Mr Kershaw. He'd only been her form tutor since the start of the year but she thought of him as someone a bit special: he wasn't quite like other teachers. Without ever having spoken to him about anything really personal, she thought he was the sort of person you could tell anything to; he would understand, would sort out your problems for you. And now, if Natalie was right, he was proving himself fallible, fickle. Wanting the flattery of a younger woman's attentions, to make him feel good about himself.

Like Dad.

Jo stared at Miss Kelland as she took off her helmet and shook out her mane of fair hair. Flushed and dishevelled, she looked about eighteen, though she must obviously be older than that to be a qualified teacher. Steve's wife was probably worn out with broken nights and the stress of looking after a baby; she'd be too tired when Steve came home to take much interest in him. Not bothering to make herself look nice...

'What's the matter with you?' Lynette gave Jo a shove. 'Standing there daydreaming. I just said, Do you think we'll see wild animals up here, deer or eagles, that sort of thing?'

'Not with us lot shrieking and yelling,' Jo said. 'I should think any deer with any sense is about fifteen miles away.'

'Judith's doing all right,' Lynette said, pointing. 'I thought she'd be scared, didn't you?'

Judith Sutherland, a shining model of virtue in the classroom, was quite timid when it came to physical activity, according to Ellie, who knew her from the riding stables. Judith didn't go riding any more, Ellie said, scared off by her experiences with a spirited pony her parents had bought her. However, Judith came down the rock face with no trouble at all. When it was Natalie's turn, she evidently decided to follow Miss Kelland's example, making the most of undivided male attention: it seemed to take Gary a very long time to adjust the harness, before Natalie came down quite smoothly. After her came Hayley, a shrieking bundle.

'OK, that's the fun bit,' Gary told them when the final four had abseiled down. 'Well done everyone. We'll do that again on Thursday, but a lot more quickly. And remember what I told you last night – abseiling may be fun, but it's also one of the most frequent causes of accidents, if people think it's *too* easy and start mucking about. It's perfectly safe if you do exactly what you're told, but if you –' he looked sternly at Sanjay '– fancy doing your Tarzan act again, keep it for the playground at school. Here, you concentrate. Now we're going to climb up, which is a bit harder.'

It had been a good day, Jo reflected as she got ready for bed that night. She had passed her first real test, and had proved to Gary that she wasn't a wimp or a whinger. The afternoon had been spent walking on the lower slopes of the Black Mountains, and the evening in learning navigation. Tomorrow, riding and putting into practice what they'd learned about orienteering...

There was just one thing wrong. It was nearly ten o'clock, and Jo, Lynette and Ellie were all just about ready for bed, but the other three from their room were nowhere to be seen.

'Not our problem,' Lynette said resolutely, drawing her duvet cover up to her ears.

'They've gone off to have a fag somewhere, I expect,' Ellie suggested. 'Better outside than in.'

'But what are we going to say when a teacher comes round?' Jo asked.

Right on cue, there was a knock at the door and Mrs Hughes' voice said, 'Everyone all right in there?'

'Yes, thanks. Goodnight,' Lynette called back, and they heard Mrs Hughes' footsteps go along the corridor.

Ellie looked anxious. She had just brushed her hair so that it stood out like a wild mane around her face (Jo envied Ellie her hair: hers would only hang straight) and her eyes looked big and dark in the rather inadequate lighting of their room. 'Was that a good idea?' she asked Lynette. 'What if they've wandered off somewhere? They might die of exposure or drown in a swamp—'

'Shame,' Jo said.

'They won't go anywhere near a swamp. They're having a fag behind those sheds outside, like you said,' Lynette said confidently. 'I'm not staying awake worrying about them. They can look after themselves.'

Some while later, the missing three turned up, tiptoeing exaggeratedly along the corridor and then, once safely inside the room, turning on the lights and talking loudly enough to bring Mrs Hughes to the door.

'I take a dim view of being woken up,' she said sternly, 'and it's time you were all asleep.' Her glance flicked over Lynette, who was somehow sleeping through the disturbance, and landed reproachfully on Jo, who had just sat up in bed to remonstrate with Natalie. 'It's only Saturday night. If you think I'm putting up with noise like this for another five nights, you've got another think coming. Now go to sleep.'

She closed the door firmly. Hayley's bed became a giggling heap, with muffled squeals of laughter coming from under the blanket.

'Now do be quiet, Jo,' Natalie said sternly. She was brilliant at impersonations, and she could do Mrs Hughes to perfection, looking at Jo over imaginary spectacles and speaking in a voice weighted with disappointed expectations. 'I've told you about this rowdy behaviour before. Some of us are trying to get to sleep.'

Gossip

'Can any of you ride?' the woman at the stables asked, looking doubtfully at the assembled group. The ponies were all saddled and ready in an open-sided barn.

'Ellie can,' Judith said.

'So can Jude,' Ellie said quickly.

'But Ellie's really good.'

'OK, then. Ellie, do you think you can manage quite a lively pony? Fun to ride, but needs a firm hand?'

'All right,' Ellie said, looking pleased at the challenge.

'You take Minstrel, then, the grey pony at the far end. And Judith, is it? You can ride too? You'd better ride Buddy, the roan. Now we'll sort out the smallest people.' She surveyed the group, picking out Craig first and allocating him to a tiny black pony with a shaggy mane.

'Oh, the cute little thing,' Hayley mocked. 'Is it a pony or a dog?'

'You're next smallest.' The woman pointed at Jo. 'You can take Dormouse, the little bay one.'

Dormouse! That didn't sound very exciting. Jo had imagined herself riding a spirited pony like the one Ellie was getting; this one looked more suitable for giving pony-rides to toddlers on a beach. It was small, fat and hairy, with a sleepy expression that suited its name.

When everyone had been fitted with helmets, one of the girl helpers showed everyone how to mount and adjust their stirrups and hold their reins. Jo's pony showed no reaction at all when she climbed on and picked up the reins, and she imagined it would be quite happy to carry on dozing while she sat on its back.

'She'll just follow the others. You'll be OK,' the girl said, as if Jo were a quivering wreck.

'I want your pony. This one's miles too big,' Lynette said, from on board a large piebald with a rolling eye that made it look aggressive. 'I'll fall off if it moves.'

'Don't pull on the reins. You'll hurt his mouth,' the woman shouted to Sanjay, who was trying to get his pony to move.

'I'm going to be so stiff after this,' Natalie

complained. 'My arms are already aching from the climbing.'

Jo thought it was strange to see everyone on ponies. Ellie and Judith, of course, looked completely at home, sitting straight and confident. Others looked as if they had no balance whatsoever, clutching wildly at saddles and manes if their ponies so much as shuffled forward. Some people looked as if their arms and legs had suddenly become unmanageable, feet sticking out, arms tense. Damien had managed to get his reins entangled into knots and wrapped round one of his feet. Steve Kershaw and Miss Kelland had gone climbing again today, with the other group, and Mrs Hughes was the teacher in charge of the riding. Astride a speckly pinkish pony, she looked a little uncertain but was trying to keep her teacherly dignity by doing everything absolutely correctly.

'You sit like this,' the Welsh woman called out. 'Relaxed. Don't stick your legs forward. Sit comfortably. The ponies know what to do, so you don't have to worry about steering them. Everyone all right?'

She led the way out of the yard along a stony track which wound gradually up into a conifer forest. Jo's Dormouse walked with quick stumpy strides, occasionally breaking into a jog trot if it began to fall behind the bigger ponies, but apart from managing to sit on it, Jo needed no equestrian skill at all. Natalie, riding one of the bigger ponies, almost a horse, called out, 'There's nothing to this, is there? Can't we go a bit faster?'

'Perhaps later,' the Welsh woman called back.

Jo looked up at Ellie, who was sitting easily on the arch-necked grey pony, her hands light on the reins. 'I thought Natalie could ride already?' Jo asked. 'Didn't she go to the stables with you and Amanda at one time?'

Ellie looked uncomfortable. 'There was something funny about it,' she said in a low voice. 'She told us she could ride but it was obvious she couldn't. And then she stopped coming.'

The woman at the front turned round in her saddle. 'Ellie? And that other girl – Judith? When the track forks in two you can take the right-hand one if you like. There's a place to canter, and a few jumps.'

'Wow! Like the Badminton Horse Trials!' Hayley called out, clutching the front of her saddle. 'Can't we all have a go?'

'I'd like to see you,' Natalie retorted. 'You'd bounce straight off like a sack of potatoes.'

Everyone watched, impressed, as Ellie and Judith overtook the other ponies and set off at a fast canter. Minstrel, Ellie's pony, was beautiful, full of controlled energy, his white mane flying as he charged eagerly at the log jumps, gathered himself and cleared them with a foot to spare. That was real riding, Jo thought, not merely being carried along by a placid pony, as she was – being able to speak the same language, almost mind-reading, as if you became one animal. Jo envied Ellie, but was glad for her to have the chance to show that she could do something really well, and something that was so good to watch, too.

'Lovely! You're a good little rider,' the woman said to Ellie when she trotted back to join the group. 'And you did the jumps nicely too,' she added to Judith, who had followed more sedately.

For the others, the only exciting part of the ride was when the whole group ventured a cautious trot along a peaty track. Shrieks and yells resounded beneath the trees as riders were jolted in their saddles, lost their stirrups and sagged over their ponies' necks. Somehow, no one fell off, although Hayley was right out of her saddle with arms clutched round her pony's neck by the time they slowed to a walk.

Lynette regained a lost stirrup and pushed her helmet out of her eyes. 'That was *horrendous*. I never want to do that again. I'm sure this evil pony wants to get its teeth into me.'

'It was a bit boring,' Natalie pronounced when the ride was over and they were back in the stable-yard. 'I thought we'd all gallop about, like Ellie did. *And here comes Miss Elena Snooty-Boots-Twitchett-Smythe, riding High and Mighty,'* she announced, in a plummy voice. *'Oh I say, she's gone A over T in the water jump – fifty-seven faults—'*

Jo looked round quickly. Ellie was leading her pony into the barn, out of earshot.

'That's not fair,' she told Natalie. 'Ellie didn't ask to ride that pony, or to go over the jumps. She's not a show-off. Just because she's miles better than any of us, there's no need to start getting at her.'

'I thought Ellie was brilliant,' said Greg Batt, whose pony had dragged him over to the water-trough.

Natalie, Lynette and Jo all turned to stare at him. Greg was a quiet, clever boy who rarely spoke unless he had to. Realising that he had become the centre of attention, he went bright red and turned away to attend to his pony.

'You what, Batman?' Natalie's face lit up with malicious interest, and Jo knew that Greg would suffer for his remark later, if not now.

'I said she's a brilliant rider, that's all.' Greg started to run his stirrups up the leathers as they'd been shown, hiding his face under the saddle flap.

'Yes, she is. I wish I could ride as well as that,' Lynette said.

'On that white pony? You fancy being the black-

and-white Minstrels?' Natalie joked. Jo looked at her sharply: that was a racist joke, wasn't it? But Lynette only laughed.

The afternoon's activity was a walk in the Black Mountains area – a short one, to get them ready for more taxing climbs later in the week. The scenery was just what Jo had imagined – tufty grass marked by sheep-tracks, purpling misty heights, valleys with thread-like streams twining through, dark clumps of trees, and in the distance, level plains of agricultural land. She had dreamed of wild places like this, her escape from roads and concrete. The only problem was that by coming with a group she had brought school with her. It was hard to ignore the tiresome jokes Damien and Sanjay were telling, Leanne's shrieks of laughter and Hayley's complaints about her blistered feet and the steepness of the path. Deliberately, she dropped back so that she could fully absorb the atmosphere. No one noticed: Lynette was talking to Judith, Ellie walking beside Greg Batt.

Soon, in spite of herself, Jo found her thoughts completely occupied with the problem of Mum. She thought of Mum alone in the shop all week, wondering if there was any point in staying open. Throwing away half the home-cooked cakes and savouries because no one was coming in to buy them.

Looking at the cash register sitting idle on its table. Contemplating failure, the dismal ending of her dream of independence. And suddenly Jo wanted more than anything to be back at home, serving in the shop with Mum, weighing out the packets of herbs and spices or arranging the walnut brownies on display. Jo could smell the cinnamon and nutmeg and cumin that pervaded the shop. If only she were there, she could help Mum to cheer up – think of some new way of displaying the stuff, devising a window display that no passer-by could resist. Nan would be back now from her Norfolk week, but she wouldn't be much help. Nan was too busy with her own shop and her Ramblers friends, and in any case if *Thinking of You* ever did face closure, it wouldn't be Nan's problem; she could simply get a job somewhere else. Nan didn't understand what the shop meant to Mum.

It was no good. Jo would have to phone home. Tonight.

Although there was a phone in the entrance hall of the lodge, phoning home wasn't as easy as it sounded. Mobile phones wouldn't work here in the valley, so everyone wanted the payphone. Between the evening meal and the session of mapwork practice, there was only about forty minutes, and anyway the phone was in too public a place to offer privacy. That evening, Jo went down with her coins ready, only to find Nathan there, his shoulders hunched furtively inside the rounded hood of the phone booth, talking urgently. Jo didn't mean to eavesdrop, but she heard him say, 'What if he doesn't?'

Jo retreated to wait by the large-scale map on the wall. It seemed odd for Nathan to be phoning home – he always struck her as the sort of person who was only too glad to get away. Perhaps he was phoning his Dad about Gaz. While she waited, staring at the map, she traced with her finger the route from the red blob which marked Penhowell, down the track and along the lane to the village. The scale was so large that every cottage and garden was marked, small rectangles inside larger ones.

There was the tramp of feet down stairs and Natalie's voice said, 'Oh, Nathan's on the phone. Hurry up, Nathe.'

All three of them came down, Natalie, Hayley and Leanne, jingling coins and crowding round Nathan. He slammed the phone down and walked off huffily, and Hayley giggled and started looking through her address book. 'Me first. I've got three calls to make.'

This was hopeless. Jo didn't want to talk to Mum with those three milling round and no doubt interrupting. Through the window, Jo saw Imogen wheeling a bike round to one of the outhouses. The map showed a telephone symbol in the village; she had just seen it. If she borrowed the bike, she could make it to the village and back before the evening session started.

She raced outside and asked Imogen if she could borrow the bike, just for half an hour.

Imogen looked doubtful, but said, 'It's OK with me, but you'll have to get permission from your teacher. I can't let you go off the premises.'

'Thanks!'

Jo went back inside and dithered in the hallway. She knew the teachers wouldn't let her go out on her own, and in any case she wasn't sure where they were. She could easily get down to the village and back before anyone noticed.

It was dusk outside, the air still, smelling of damp earth and fresh growth. Jo pushed the bike out of sight of the building and then set off, riding as fast as she could between the stone walls of the lane. The bike's headlamp caught moths and darting flies in its beam. The phone box, beside the pub, was fortunately unoccupied.

'Mum, it's me. How are you?'

'Oh, I'm fine, thanks. How are *you*? How's it going?'

Mum didn't sound as if she'd been weeping over her accounts, but Jo was sure she recognised her putting-a-brave-face-on-it voice. However, Mum would only talk about what Jo was doing. They talked until Jo's money ran out, and then Jo went out to the bike, not altogether reassured. Perhaps it was *Dad* she should have phoned, to ask him to go round and see Mum and cheer her up; but she had no change left now. Besides, she needed to talk to Dad first herself, so that he knew exactly what to say and do. She felt wearied by the weight of her problems. Her arms and legs ached from the riding and the climbing, and even the few minutes' standing still in the phone box had made her muscles tighten up.

A vehicle was coming towards her. She moved towards the verge, then saw that it was slowing, stopping. In the light of her headlamp she saw that it was a red van with the letters PENHOWELL OUTDOOR PURSUITS CENTRE in white along the sides. A window wound down and the driver's face looked out at her.

Mr Kershaw. And Miss Kelland was in the passenger seat.

'Jo? What the hell do you think you're doing?'

'I just borrowed Imogen's bike, to go to the phone box,' Jo said, wanting to ask *What the hell do you think YOU'RE doing?* Where were they going, the two of them?

'Oh, you *just*,' Mr Kershaw repeated sarcastically. 'Useful word, isn't it, *just*? I suppose you didn't *just* think of mentioning it, or even *just* asking if it was all right with us? Because, for your information, it *just* isn't. Do you think we can have pupils wandering around the lanes in the dark, without any of the staff having a clue where they are?'

'No. Sorry. But I wasn't wandering,' Jo said. 'I was on my way back.'

'Why didn't you use the phone box in the hall?'

'There was a queue.' There was no point trying to excuse herself; she knew she was in the wrong.

'Oh, I *see*. There was a queue. Well, that makes it all right, then.'

Mr Kershaw wasn't usually sarcastic, and Jo didn't like it now.

'Sorry,' she said again.

'Sorry. "Sorry," she says.' He turned exasperatedly to Miss Kelland, then back to Jo. 'Do you realise what a difficult position you've put us in? Imagine if there were some emergency – a fire, say – and we had to evacuate the building, with no one knowing where you were?'

'Yes. I do realise.' She couldn't keep saying sorry, so she asked instead, 'Have you come out specially to look for me?'

'No. Er – we're on our way somewhere else.' Mr Kershaw looked rather embarrassed. 'Get straight back to the Centre, Jo, and don't do anything so stupid again. This course is about responsibility as much as anything else. Remember that.'

He gave her a parting nod, slipped the car into gear and drove on. Jo watched as the red tail-lights moved slowly away, stopped outside the pub and then faded as the engine was switched off. Both Steve and Miss Kelland got out and went inside.

Jo stood there in disbelief, staring at the closed pub door. How blatant could you get? Natalie had obviously been right about those two. Sloping off to spend the evening in the pub, while everyone else went to the orienteering practice! And then having the cheek to talk about *responsibility*...

'Huh! It's not *me* who needs to be more responsible!' she told the empty lane.

'He what?' Lynette whispered back.

'Went to the pub with Miss Kelland. It wasn't rubbish, what Natalie said. They *are* having an affair.'

Lynette was poring over her map with a compass in one hand and a pen in the other, working out approximate timings for an ascent. Glancing up, she said, 'They can't have spent long there, then. Here they are.'

Jo looked towards the doorway. Mr Kershaw and Miss Kelland were coming in, not looking in the least furtive or guilty. They separated, joining different groups of pupils and looking at the task set. Steve Kershaw came over to Lynette's group.

'It's obvious who's doing all the work here,' he said, meaning Lynette. 'All right, Cannonball? Raring to get at those canoes tomorrow?'

It was his way of saying that the telling-off in the lane was all forgotten. But Jo wasn't in the mood to forgive him.

'Yes, thank you,' she said coolly.

The orienteering part of the course was to lead up to a team competition on the last day, with prizes for the winners. Mr Kershaw had forbidden bargaining over who was going with who, saying that he would be choosing the teams, but now an announcement was being made for the next day's activity.

'Pairs for canoes,' Imogen announced, holding up a list. 'No changing around. Natalie, Damien. Sanjay, Lynette. Greg, Ellie. Nathan, Jo...'

'Bad luck,' Natalie said to Jo across the table, loudly enough for Nathan to hear.

'What bad luck?' Jo retaliated. 'We'll be a good team, won't we, Nathan?'

Nathan gave one of his unintelligible grunts, and Natalie turned her attention to Greg and Ellie, who happened to be sitting next to each other and had both gone a bit pink and embarrassed.

'Well. You two are becoming quite an item,' she

said sweetly. 'I hope Luke Flynn won't be jealous, Ellie.'

Ellie turned brighter pink, and Greg suddenly became engrossed in his orienteering notes.

Sgwds

'Most people who fall in the water do it while they're getting in or out of their canoes,' Imogen said, standing on the river bank. 'And it's pretty cold at this time of year. Not recommended.'

The canoes had been brought to the riverside on a special trailer and had been unloaded. Jo thought they looked frighteningly light and fragile, especially when she looked at the greenish waters of the River Wye, which was running strongly with eddies and currents swirling. She had visions of being swept all the way down to the Severn Estuary and out to the Atlantic. With Nathan.

Judith was the envy of most of the girls this morning, because she was sharing a canoe with Gary. 'Must be because Imogen thinks Jude's too wet to manage without her own personal instructor,' Natalie decided. Imogen herself was sharing with Scott, who Natalie said needed someone nearly as light as himself or the canoe would sink down at the other end.

As with everything else, they had been told the safety procedures beforehand, and had been fitted with life-jackets over their waterproof coats. Although the sun was shining, there was a cold wind, especially at river level. The canoe trip was quite straightforward, downstream to an allotted point where Mr Kershaw would meet them with the trailer, and the only real hazard – once they were safely in their canoes – would be low-growing branches at the river's edge.

Imogen floated the canoes into the water and held each one steady while the two occupants climbed gingerly in, sat down and organised their paddles. Jo took the front seat, remembering that Nathan at the back would have the main job of steering, and that basically all she had to do was to keep paddling. At first she made big splashes, but then found it easy to slip the paddle into the water and pull.

'Keep to the centre,' Imogen shouted from time to time. 'Lynette, don't let yourself drift over to the bank. There's overhanging trees round the next bend.'

As long as you had a reliable person to steer – and Nathan proved to be surprisingly reliable, though he hardly spoke – there was nothing difficult about it. Jo had time to admire the surroundings: at first houses, with gardens sloping right down to the water's edge; then thick woods with occasional clearings and glimpses of a footpath. Then, an island which had to be steered round. The channels each side narrowed and darkened, and the canoe sped through on the current to a calmer, wider stretch of water with gravelly shallows and low-growing willow trees, showing the first pale shadings of new leaves.

Jo was concentrating on the next bend, saying, 'A bit to the right here, Nathan,' when a shriek from behind made them both turn round. Hayley and Leanne had somehow drifted right under the trees, and were leaning backwards in their canoes in an attempt to avoid getting the branches in their faces.

'Oh, my paddle!' Leanne yelled.

Imogen, ahead, made her canoe spin round to face upstream, by which time the two girls had emerged from under the willows, and Leanne was reaching out for the floating paddle. 'OK – nearly got it—' she called to Hayley, when suddenly there was a muffled scream and the canoe rolled right over, obscuring both girls. It flipped back, empty, and started to float downstream.

Jo looked at Imogen, half-expecting her to dive to the rescue, but instead Imogen was going after the escaping canoe and paddle. Hayley and Leanne struggled and spluttered and stood upright, dripping and trailing weed, in no more than three feet of water. As soon as everyone realised they weren't in danger of drowning, there were shrieks of laughter and shouted jokes from everyone in sight.

'Yow, it's freezing!' Leanne wailed.

'Don't just sit there laughing,' Hayley snapped at Natalie and Damien, who had wheeled round to enjoy the fun. 'Help us get out!'

'Hasn't anyone got a camera?' Natalie shouted.

Between them, Imogen and Gary caught the empty canoe and pulled it over the bank, turned it over to a great gush of water, and held it ready for Leanne and Hayley to get back in.

Hayley stared at them incredulously. 'You're kidding! Get back *in*? After being frozen and half-drowned?'

'Best way to get warm. You can't wait here,' Gary pointed out.

'Oh, my *hair*,' Leanne wailed, holding out dripping handfuls. 'I only washed and blow-dried it this morning.'

No one else managed to fall in. When they reached the bend in the river where Mr Kershaw was to meet them, Hayley and Leanne were sent straight back to the Centre for hot baths, while everyone else had a free hour and a half in Hay-on-Wye. Natalie, deprived of her usual companions, attached herself to Lynette, Jo and Ellie, and they went together to a café for Cokes and ice-cream.

'That was great, wasn't it? Those two pratts capsizing?' Natalie said with satisfaction, leaning back in her chair. 'One of the best stories of the week. Wait till we tell everyone else back at school.'

'Getting sent back with Gary in the van might be some consolation,' Lynette said, picking bits of chocolate off her choc-ice.

'Except that he was laughing at them,' Natalie pointed out. 'I bet they expected Tender Loving Care. Gary personally running hot baths for them.'

'He must be used to it,' Jo said. 'People probably fall in every week.'

'What shall we do now?' Lynette asked.

'Mr Kershaw said there are about a hundred second-hand bookshops here,' Jo said. 'I'm going to see if I can find something for Mum.'

'I'll come with you,' Natalie said, to Jo's surprise. 'Darren's doing AS English. I might get something for him.'

Lynette and Ellie quickly decided that they were going to a craft shop they'd seen on the way, and hurried off before Natalie could change her mind and go with them. Jo and Natalie went into the nearest bookshop, which had racks of books on the pavement (didn't people *steal* them?) and consisted, inside, of corridors and corners and flights of stairs in unexpected places, with shelves of dusty books reaching right up to the ceiling.

'I don't know where to start,' Natalie said. 'Perhaps I'd be better off finding W. H. Smith's. This stuff looks like it came out of the Ark. What do you reckon?'

'English Literature, this way.' Jo pointed to a cardboard sign and arrow pinned to the wall, and after going up two more wooden staircases, down half a level and round two corners they came to a small room full of the sort of stuff Mum was reading for her course – novels, poetry, literary criticism. Some of the books were horrendously expensive, considering how tatty they were, but at last she chose a cloth-bound copy of *The Professor* by Charlotte Brontë; she didn't think Mum had that one. Natalie was picking books off the shelves and putting them back again without any idea what she was looking for, so Jo suggested a paperback volume of *The Penguin Guide to English Literature*. She'd seen that on the kitchen table at home, and assumed it must be a generally useful sort of book.

'No bag, thanks,' Jo said to the man at the till downstairs.

'Why not?' Natalie asked.

'It's a waste of packaging. Waste of paper. I never have bags from shops if I don't need them. Think of all the bags that get thrown away when you don't need them in the first place.'

'OK, then. I forgot you were a Greenie,' Natalie said, without making something snidey out of it, the way she usually would. 'No bag for me either,' Natalie told the shopkeeper. Out in the street, she said, 'Thanks, Jo. I wouldn't have had a clue what to get. This was a good idea.'

'That's OK.' Jo was sometimes surprised by how nice Natalie could be. 'What do you want to do now? We've got another fifteen minutes.'

'See you back at the coach. I've just remembered something,' Natalie said, and ran off across the road before Jo could ask what, or offer to go with her.

Jo thought the next two days were fantastic.

('You shouldn't *say* fantastic unless you really mean it,' Jo's mum had announced recently, when Jo had been enthusiastic about a new recipe. 'That's one of the first things our tutor told us. We should stop mauling the language about and use it properly, he says. *Fantastic* doesn't just mean *good*. It means – well, like something out of a fantasy.' And she went and fetched the dictionary, to be quite sure what it *did* mean. 'Listen. *Fantastic*. Unbelievable – no, that's another word people bandy about. Oddly elaborate, grotesque, eccentric. So if you say my asparagus quiche is fantastic again, I shall take it as an insult.'

'But you've got to admit, that quiche *is* a bit eccentric,' Jo pointed out, earning a swipe with the dictionary.)

Like something out of a fantasy. Well, if that were one of the meanings of *fantastic*, she felt quite justified in using the word. The waterfall walk, travelling by coach to the Nedd Gorge and then spending the whole day walking through steep ravines, beside rushing rivers and waterfalls with weird names like Squid Gladys. That was how Steve pronounced the names, at least, but Gary, a Welsh speaker, said it was really Sgwd Gwladys and Sgwd yr Eira. Sgwd meant waterfall, and Sgwd yr Eira meant Waterfall of the Snow.

'We're going to walk round *behind* this one,' Gary explained. 'And if anyone falls in I won't be diving in to save them, so go carefully, strictly single file, and *no messing about*. Did you hear that, Damien? It's a bit slippery, so take care.'

A rocky path led down to Sgwyd yr Eira and round behind what looked like a solid wall of sliding water, like liquid glass. The force threw up a fine spray which Jo could smell and taste. The party inched carefully forward, led by Gary. The noise of the waterfall became a roaring in Jo's ears as she stepped over the dark, slippery rock into a cavern behind, and smelled damp rock and fern. Looking at the curtain of water made her dizzy – gazing up at the slide into space, a river throwing itself off a cliff. Ahead, the mesmerising downward drop of the column of water. She walked carefully to the other side, where she gazed down at the purity of white spray, the swirl and eddy of water against rock.

'Awesome!' said Damien.

Another word Jo's mum objected to. But it was.

And next day, climbing, climbing, legs aching, lungs protesting, shoulders aching with rucksack-weight, up the valley and out to the ridge, higher and higher. Far above the cottages and farms, above trees, above all vegetation except turf and bog grass blown like hair by the wind. To the summits of Pen y Fan and Corn Du, where the edge was scalloped away as if scooped out by a giant's teaspoon, to reveal striated layers of rock below dropping sheer, down to the valley. The track down, to a standing stone in a circle of peat; everyone sitting round, like infants at story time, listening to Gary's sad story about the boy Tommy Jones who had wandered up into the hills and died there of exposure. Mountains were dangerous; the instructors repeated that time and time again, you could die of hypothermia even in summer if you weren't properly equipped. But the mountains didn't feel dangerous today. Their slopes were like the fleeces of benign slumbering animals, giant creatures from Welsh legend deep in sleep, their hides flecked with sun and cloud.

Back on the coach:

'Fantastic!'

'That slog up nearly killed me.'

'Have we really been all the way up *there?*'

'I've got a blister the size of a melon on one of my heels.'

'It was even better than those Sgwds yesterday.'

Jo wanted to come and live here. She wanted the mountains for her back garden.

'Tomorrow afternoon, the orienteering team challenge,' Steve Kershaw announced impressively at the end of dinner. 'Here are the teams. *Absolutely no changing about.* We've worked this out very carefully.'

Jo was in a team with Hayley, Nathan and Scott. This, she decided glumly, gave her absolutely no chance of winning. Hayley did nothing except grumble and trail along at the pace of a tortoise in low gear – she wouldn't have got up Pen y Fan today without being coaxed, cajoled and almost shoved up by Mrs Hughes. Scott was hopelessly vague and always left decisions to other people; Nathan was totally unpredictable. It crossed Jo's mind that Mr Kershaw was getting his own back on her by putting her in such a hopeless team, since he claimed to have worked things out so carefully. They sat in their groups round tables while he, Gary and Imogen handed out laminated maps and instructions. Jo looked enviously across at Lynette, who had landed in a group with Judith, Greg and Damien. Damien could be an idiot sometimes but he was a fast and fit walker and would be determined to win, and the other three all had brains.

'You've got nine points to find, starting from here, all shown on the map,' Gary explained. 'Usually some sort of landmark – for instance the first one's a disused barn. At each one there's a red-and-white post with a letter painted on it. You've got to write down that letter to prove you've been there – so when you come back, you show us your list, 1J, 2X or whatever. The distance you'll cover is six miles. Listen to this bit carefully and follow what I'm saying on your maps. You might wander off course, but you can't get into trouble *providing* you don't cross the lane to the village at the bottom of the map – it's got stone walls, so you can't cross it without noticing – or the dirt track at the left and top, or on the east side, the double stone wall going straight up to the hills. That means you stay within the marked area and if anyone gets into trouble we can easily come and find you. Everyone got that?'

'Six *miles*?' Hayley muttered, next to Jo. 'We've got to walk another six miles? I'm half-dead after today.'

'Shut up and listen,' Jo said curtly. She anticipated putting up with Hayley's grumbles all tomorrow afternoon. She wasn't going to start now.

'You're treating it as an expedition. So you've got a compass per team, your map, of course, and a whistle. Everyone carries their own rucksack with a warm sweater, your waterproofs if you've not already got them on, and some food and drink. The teams must stay together, unless of course someone sprains their ankle or something – we've already told you how to organise yourself in that sort of emergency. Hopefully there won't *be* any emergencies. We start you off at fifteen-minute intervals and the team to complete the course in the shortest time wins.'

'What's the prize?' Damien asked.

'Oh – er—' Gary looked round at Steve Kershaw, who said, 'Something absolutely magnificent,' which Jo took to mean he hadn't thought about it yet. 'You know it's not the prize that counts. It's the glory of winning.'

'Some glory,' Hayley mumbled.

'*You* needn't worry,' Jo said. 'I can't see us winning unless all the other teams fall down a ravine or disappear into a time-warp.'

'Perhaps it'll pour with rain tomorrow and we won't go,' Scott suggested hopefully.

'Oh, we'll go all right.' Jo was sure of that. 'Rain, snow or heatwave. All part of the fun.'

'I'm going to be ill tomorrow. I've decided,' Hayley said. 'I can feel it coming on now.'

Upstairs in their room, Natalie had decided that her team was going to win. She was in a group with Sanjay, Leanne and a boy called Tom from another form who did a lot of hill-walking with his family and was ace at the map-and-compass work.

'Don't worry. We'll share the prize with you, won't we, Lee? Chocolate Easter eggs, that's what it'll be,' Natalie predicted.

Hayley wouldn't be consoled. 'It's not fair. I'm not bothering to go. You're bound to win, so what's the point?'

'You've got Jo on your team. She's pretty good,' Natalie said.

'Don't forget about my lot.' Lynette turned round from cleaning her teeth. 'We're in with a chance.'

'You've got Nathan and Scott,' Natalie teased

Hayley. 'You can have some interesting conversations while you trudge round. They're both so witty and fascinating.'

Hayley threw her hairbrush down on her bunk. 'Sometimes I hate you, Nat. You still haven't stopped going on about that stupid canoe trip. And you can hardly wait to spread it all round the school the minute we're back. I suppose you're dying for me to come last tomorrow as well.'

Natalie lay back on her bunk and reached into her bag. 'Don't get your knickers in a twist. I haven't shown you what I bought the other day, have I? This'll cheer you up.'

She lifted out a slim bottle with a white label.

Leanne leaned over to look, and gave a shriek of surprise. 'Vodka! When did you get that?'

'In Hay-on-Wye the other day. In the supermarket. They didn't even ask my age,' Natalie said, tossing her hair back.

'Are you mad?' Lynette said scornfully. 'You're not going to drink that, are you?'

'Drink it?' Natalie held the bottle in front of her, pretending to realise for the first time what it was for. 'Well, what a good idea, now you mention it. Better than washing my hair with it, don't you think?'

Jo was sitting on her bunk in her pyjamas with the things she needed for tomorrow spread around her rucksack. 'You know the rules about school trips. You'd be up in front of the Head for that, even suspended.'

'No one's going to know, are they? That's why I got vodka. It doesn't smell on your breath,' Natalie said. 'Anyway, I wasn't going to offer it to you three Miss Goody Two Shoeses—'

'Goody Six Shoes?' Lynette queried.

Natalie glared at her. '—it's too expensive to waste.'

Ellie, already in bed, turned her face to the wall holding her book close to her face, withdrawing herself from the conversation. Jo glanced at Lynette.

'It's not fair to us if you drink it in here,' Lynette said. 'We don't want to be involved.'

'Oh no, you wouldn't soil your lips with even one little sip, would you?' Natalie said in her most patronising voice.

'I've tasted vodka at home and I don't like it,' Lynette said. She turned her back, arranging her duvet and pillow.

'It's an acquired taste,' Natalie said, unscrewing the bottle. 'For adults. When I go out with Darren I have it with orange.' She took a deep swig, wiped the top and passed it to Hayley, who giggled and drank and then reached over to Leanne.

'Sounds vile,' Jo remarked.

Natalie held out the bottle to her. 'You ever tasted vodka, Jo?'

'No.'

'Go on, taste it then. Just a little sip.'

Jo hesitated, long enough for curiosity to get the better of her. One little sip wouldn't really implicate her in Natalie's drinking session. One little sip wasn't the same as going out and buying the stuff, or smuggling it into the Lodge.

She took the bottle and tilted it until the liquid touched her lips, and let the tiniest amount into her mouth. The spirity fumes of it filled her mouth and nose, making her want to sneeze. She swallowed, noticing Lynette's look of reproach. It was a bit like swallowing paraffin; she didn't think she would ever like it.

'That's all. I only wanted a taste,' she defended herself. 'I'm not having any more.'

Natalie giggled, lighting up a cigarette. 'Too right you're not. Give it back here.' She took the bottle and went over to the window, opening it wide to lean out.

Lynette climbed into bed in a bustly sort of way, glaring at Jo. 'Are you mad? Suppose Mrs Hughes had come in just then?' she hissed.

'Well, she didn't!'

'You want to watch out, Jo. Hughsie's already got you down as a troublemaker,' Natalie teased. She took another swig of vodka and passed it with her cigarettes and lighter to Hayley.

Jo decided that Lynette did have a point. 'Are you going to drink that whole bottle?' she asked Natalie. 'Because if you're going to be sick in the middle of the night, I don't want to be woken up.'

'That's all right,' Natalie said. 'We're used to drinking, aren't we, Hay? Oh dear, I haven't offered any to Ellie,' she added as if talking to an infant. 'Come on, Ellie, get your nose out of that book and have some booze and a fag. It's time you got a bit more practice in. What are you reading, anyway?'

'It's about the First World War,' Ellie said over her shoulder, still holding the book up to her face.

Natalie shrieked with laughter. 'First World War! You really know how to rock and roll, don't you? I suppose you and Batman have long conversations about it. At least it gives you something to talk about.'

'Give it a rest, Natalie,' Ellie said, hunching a shoulder to form a barricade. 'Can't you see I'm trying to read? And no thanks, I don't want any of your drink. You can leave me out.'

Jo, who had been about to say, 'Leave her alone,' exchanged a surprise glance with Lynette, seeing that there was no need to. Natalie just shrugged, losing interest. Ellie was learning to stand up to her at last.

'Hey, I nearly forgot,' Natalie announced. 'I've got something else in my bag as well. Nicked it from my dad.' She delved in the bottom and pulled out a miniature bottle of whisky. 'Want some of this, Hay?'

Jo dumped her rucksack on the floor and got into bed. Definitely time to crash out.

Teamwork

'Natalie, wake up. Natalie, *wake up!*'

Leanne gave a poke, a prod, then a shove. Natalie struggled up on to one elbow, blinking blearily.

'Yeah, yeah, *OK*. What's all the fuss?'

Jo and Lynette were already up and dressed, waiting for Ellie to come back from the shower. Hayley was still a sleeping hump, concealed entirely beneath her duvet.

'Here's Ellie. Let's go,' Lynette said, with relief. 'If those three get down to breakfast on time it'll be a miracle,' she added on the landing. 'We'll have to hope they leave the room reasonably tidy for once.'

'Some chance,' Jo said. They had already been hauled back upstairs by an irate Mrs Hughes on two occasions to put their room in order. Mrs Hughes wasn't interested in *whose* socks, hairbrushes, knickers and magazines were scattered across the floor. Keeping the room tidy was a group responsibility, as far as she was concerned.

Ellie paused on the stairs and looked round furtively. 'What about those bottles – that vodka and stuff?'

'That's one thing they *will* tidy away,' Lynette said drily. 'Natalie's obviously an old hand at that sort of thing.'

'Do you think they drank the whole lot?' Jo wondered.

Lynette gave her a scathing look. 'You did your bit to help.'

'Oh come on, Lyn. One tiny sip,' Jo defended herself. 'Hardly the same as swigging back a whole bottle.'

Ellie nudged her, noticing Steve Kershaw standing in the entrance hall looking at the map. He looked up at the sound of their hushed voices.

'Morning, girls. Looks like you'll need your wet gear for this afternoon. It's starting to rain already.'

'Great.' Jo imagined herself dragging a wet, reluctant and grumbling Hayley round the orienteering course. But then she thought of the bright side: Hayley might still be in bed by then.

There was a choice for the morning: rock-climbing or a second session of canoeing. 'The climbing will be a little bit more difficult this time,' Gary explained, 'so those of you who didn't enjoy it last time might be better off going with Imogen.' There was no choice as far as Jo was concerned: you could only go rock-climbing where there were cliffs and mountains, and the mountains were the reason she had come.

Jo loved it: the way climbing absorbed every part of her mind and body, her concentration devoted to the next handhold, the next stretch to a tiny bit of ledge. Although she was safely roped, the sense of danger still provided an extra thrill when she looked down past the edge of her boot, down the rock face over the distance she had climbed, already impressive. The rain-showers which chased each other across the valley added to the exhilaration, spattering cold drops into her face as she looked up towards the outcrop she was aiming for. She would do it. She understood now that it wasn't a matter of being scared or not scared, of being good at it or not. You simply did it because it was possible to do it, because your instructor said so. To make a fuss would be to let yourself down. She finished the last easy scramble to the crag, dizzied by the change in perspective as her eyes adjusted from the few feet of grey slate in front of her nose to the remoteness of grassy plateau, distant blue summits and shifting cloudscapes.

After lunch, final instructions were given for the

Great Orienteering Challenge, and the first group set off. If the weather held, there was to be an outdoor barbecue instead of the evening meal indoors.

Jo got her ill-assorted group together, trying her best to enthuse them with some sort of competitive spirit. Scott was completely vague about the whole proceedings; Nathan seemed to be brooding with silent anger; Hayley, who had managed to complete the morning's canoeing without getting wet, looked pale and droopy. They were due to set off last, which Jo felt just about put the lid on her chance of getting through the afternoon with any degree of dignity: her group would come in about an hour and a half after everyone else, probably halfway through the barbecue as well, if Hayley were allowed to dictate the pace. And they'd been told enough times that a group had to go at the pace of its slowest member, which with Hayley in tow meant the pace of a particularly lethargic snail.

'OK. Team number eight. Off you go!' Gary was measuring their departure time with a stop-watch, though Jo thought he might as well use a calendar in their case.

The first leg was easy. All they had to do was follow their compass-bearing across the shoulder of the field nearest the Lodge, and they could already see the sagging slate barn ahead of them, two fields away. As they walked through the long grass towards it, Jo thought about team strategy. If anyone was going to hold this team together, it would have to be her. And that meant giving everyone something to do.

'You're good at maths, Nathe,' she began, handing him her notebook and pencil. This wasn't strictly true, but she had decided that flattery was her best weapon. 'If you do the calculations each time, you can write them down here, so's we don't forget. Scott, how about you counting the paces if we need to? I'll have the map, and Hayley, once we start off each time you could keep a check with the compass.'

'I don't see why we have to bother with all that map and compass stuff,' Hayley complained. 'We can see where we're going, without all that.'

'It won't all be this easy,' Jo explained patiently. 'The next one's a junction of two streams. And this cloud's coming down.'

'I feel sick. I've already been sick once this morning,' Hayley mumbled, looking down at her feet. She hardly bothered to lift them, dragging her boots through the long grass. Anyone would be tired, walking like that, Jo thought.

'Well, we know why *that* is,' she said sharply.

'No, you don't. It's the food. It's been really gross all week.'

'Shut up moaning, Hay,' Nathan said, the first time he'd spoken. 'Who wants to listen to you droning on?'

'Oh yeah? Sorry for speaking!' Hayley flared up. She stopped walking and glared at Nathan. 'I never asked to come on this stupid walk with you, nerd-features.'

Nathan was wearing that sharp, dangerous expression which Jo recognised – it meant he could say anything, do anything. 'You think I wanted to be with you, you fat cow?' he jeered.

Hayley's lower jaw jutted. 'Listen to big mouth. We all know why your mum paid for you to come. So she could get rid of you for a week, and have lover-boy round to stay. That's what Natalie says,' she added triumphantly.

Nathan's face registered shock, pain, anger, in swift succession. Then he shouted, 'What does Natalie know, the stupid bitch?' And he flung down Jo's notebook and pencil, and ran up the hill towards the barn, long strides covering the ground with surprising speed.

'Oo-*oooo*-ooh,' Hayley hooted after him, in her annoying winding-up way.

Jo turned on Hayley, furious. 'Brilliant. Thanks a lot. Now look what you've done. Did you *have* to start on him, before we're even out of sight of the Lodge?'

'He started it, didn't he?' Hayley retaliated. 'Calling me a fat cow! I'm not supposed to mind that, I suppose?'

'He only told you to stop moaning. And he's got a point. We haven't even gone half a mile yet and we've split up.'

'He's just having a strop,' Hayley said. 'Big kid.'

Scott was standing patiently, kicking at a tuft of grass, waiting for the dispute to be resolved.

'Come on,' Jo said. 'Let's catch him up. And no more arguing, *please*.'

'Do you have to be so bossy?' Hayley grumbled, walking on with maddening slowness.

Jo matched her pace for a short while, then got fed up with waiting and strode on towards the barn. Nathan had completely disappeared – inside, she presumed. The map-and-compass work was a cinch, Jo thought, compared to the difficulties of trying to keep her team on speaking terms with each other. She'd deserve a diplomacy medal if she got round with this lot.

As she neared it, she could see that the barn was open on one side and completely roofless. She climbed over the pile of jumbled slate which had tipped down across the doorway. Inside, it was the sort of barn that had a ground floor for animals and an upper storey for hay and straw. There was a mouldering ladder leading up to a dangerous-looking floor, overhung with wet, mildewy hay. She looked up and saw Nathan sitting up there, hunched and resentful, like a brooding owl.

Jo went halfway up the ladder. 'Come down, Nathan, *please*. It's not safe up there. I know Hayley gets on your nerves but we've got to get round somehow.'

What would she do if he refused to budge? Go back to the Lodge and get one of the staff to come and fetch him? Give up, at this stage? But Nathan glared down at her, and then began to move, stretching out a long leg, groping for the ladder.

'She's a stupid bitch,' he fired at Jo as he came down.

'OK, you've got a point. But we've got to put up with her. Teamwork and all that. Come on, we've done the first bit, and –' She glanced round, and saw the red-and-white post leaning against an inside corner of the barn '– there's our first letter, Q. Write that down, then we'll work out the next bit.'

She could see various stream beds, twining down to a boggy hollow. To her relief, Nathan began to take an interest, looking closely at the map. Hayley and Scott caught up, and Hayley flashed a totally insincere smile at Nathan, which he ignored.

'Got to cross the stream at the right place,' he said,

tracing the stream on the map. 'There's more than one. Give me the compass,' he added, stretching out a hand without looking at Hayley.

They found their way without difficulty to the stream and a rudimentary bridge of slates, with the next marker point wedged beside. Now, uphill to cairns and a lightning tree. The cloud was thickening, dark and rain-filled, turning this open upland into a weird, enclosed world. Rain spattered, becoming heavier. They stopped to put on kagoules, and Jo shivered as she looked at the gaunt shape of the lightning tree. Lightning on high ground was one thing she *was* scared of.

When they reached the cairn, Hayley sat down and rummaged in her rucksack, saying she was thirsty.

'Can't you wait a bit longer?' Jo asked, anxiously checking her watch. 'We're not halfway round yet.'

'Just a quick drink. You've got to do the working-out yet anyway.'

'OK then, Nathan. That stream junction next.' She and Nathan had virtually taken over, the other two merely trailing along, but she still handed over the compass to Hayley with the new bearing set. 'Just over a kilometre to marker number three, on a bearing of 57 degrees. That's about eighteen minutes.'

'Can't use Naismith's Rule here,' Nathan said quietly to her as they set off. 'It's Hayley's Rule. One kilometre every two hours. With two sulks per contour of ascent.'

Jo laughed, surprised. It was the first time she'd heard Nathan make a joke. He grinned at her and she realised that she'd rarely, if ever, seen him smile before. He was quite nice-looking, really, with those dark brown eyes; it was just that his usual sharp, closed-in expression made him look surly and unapproachable, even thuggish. Interesting, she thought, the way you saw people away from school. If she and Nathan could do the course without the other two, they'd make a good team.

The next stream crossing was more difficult. They could see the marker post, in the middle of a boggy confluence, and Nathan wrote down the letter N. But the recent heavy rain made it difficult to get across. The banks were steep and slippery, the stream too wide to jump or wade across. They had to pick their way upstream and find a place where they could slither down the bank and jump from one boulder to another. Hayley, much to her resentment, had to submit to being helped across by Nathan.

Jo looked at the map. 'Up the stream to a bridge and track next. Well, that should be easy, but we'd better check. Give us the compass, Hay.'

Hayley felt in one pocket of her waterproof, then

another. She screwed up her face, biting her bottom lip.

'Can't find it. I know I had it back there, when you gave it to me—'

'You haven't *lost* it!' Jo rolled her eyes upwards. Hayley's only responsibility was to look after the compass; you'd think *anyone* could manage that. 'When did you last look at it? You're supposed to have been checking our direction all the way from that cairn!'

'Can't remember.' Hayley shrugged, as if it didn't matter much. 'Somewhere between here and there, I s'pose.'

'Now what?' Jo appealed to Nathan. 'Do we go back and look for it, or carry on without?'

'Not much chance,' Nathan said, indicating the marshy ground where a compass could easily sink from sight.

They cast around, trying to follow their trail, but so many others had walked this way that it seemed a hopeless task.

'We can manage without, can't we?' Hayley had been trudging along as moodily as if the loss of the compass had been nothing to do with her. 'Or do you think we ought to go back?'

It occurred to Jo that maybe Hayley had lost the compass on purpose, so that they'd have to give up.

If so, she must have little idea how much a compass would cost – it had been a proper Silva one belonging to the Centre, with a magnifier, ruler and cord, not some cheap thing. And if Hayley *had* done it deliberately, then Jo was all the more determined to continue.

'What d'you think?' she asked the others. 'Can we try to manage without?'

She and Nathan looked at the map, and decided that it would be fairly simple to find their way to the next bridge, from which point the route started to turn back towards the Centre. They set off, following the stream, skirting the boggiest bits. Jo tried to shrug off her misgivings that the cloud was coming in lower and that visibility was really very poor. The stream would guide them. Apart from the peaty trickle over boulders, she could see very little else apart from tufts of moor grass, an occasional startled sheep and the blanketing cloud. The rain was starting to come down harder, no longer in fitful bursts but in a steady downpour. Jo trod in an unexpectedly deep patch, floundered, and got a bootful of water. She tried to reassure herself that they couldn't go seriously wrong, not if they stayed within the perimeters shown on the map. Nathan was in front, walking steadily, hood up and shoulders hunched; occasionally, when Hayley and Scott lagged behind, Jo shouted at him to wait.

By now, in this mist, it was crucial that they stayed together and didn't let anyone stray off.

Eventually, Nathan stopped walking and asked to see the map. 'We should have come to the bridge by now,' he told Jo. 'According to that rule. It was less than a kilometre but we've taken more than twenty minutes. We haven't passed it.'

'Must be the boggy ground slowing us down,' Jo suggested.

'S'pose. But I hope we get to it in a minute.'

They plodded on. It occurred to Jo that as they went further upstream, there was no need for a bridge, since you could now cross easily with one stride; but then she remembered that the bridge was shown where the stream crossed a Land-Rover track. Their path was taking them uphill now, the gradient enough to make Hayley and Scott slow down considerably. Jo made sure she kept them well in sight without letting Hayley catch up enough to start grumbling. She couldn't honestly have said she was enjoying herself at this moment, with both feet wet and the wind lashing the rain into her face. And it was getting harder to see where they were supposed to be going. The ground was still boggy, in spite of the slope, the whole area interspersed with streamlets so that it became impossible to see which one they were supposed to be following.

Then Nathan stopped again. 'This isn't right.' He had taken over the map. 'We shouldn't be going uphill like this. Wherever we are, we've missed the bridge.'

Jo leaned over to look where he was pointing. The laminated surface of the map was spattered with raindrops.

'See? The contour lines aren't close enough for a hill like this,' Nathan said.

'But how can we have gone wrong? We followed the stream.'

'Are you sure you two know what you're doing?' Hayley called out, stomping through the bog to reach them.

'No. We don't,' Jo said fiercely. 'Because it's a bit difficult in a mist without a compass.'

'I think we should go back,' Hayley said plaintively. 'And so does Scott.'

Jo tightened the drawstring of her hood. 'We can't go back until we know where we are.'

'Why can't we go back the way we've come?'

'Shut up a minute and let's think,' Nathan snapped.

Jo looked at her watch. Ten past four. They ought to be arriving back at the Lodge in about ten minutes from now. Instead of which they were marooned in a bog with no idea where to go next.

'Got it,' Nathan said. 'Here's where we screwed up.

When we left that last checkpoint, we thought we were going up here, this stream. But instead we went up *this* one. There's the bridge, over there. We've come right over this way. Much too far. Somehow we've crossed the track.'

'How can we have? The one Gary told us not to cross?' Hayley mocked.

'Because we were so busy looking for the bridge.' Jo cast her mind back. 'We did cross a sort of track, didn't we?'

'I noticed it,' Scott said. 'But I didn't say anything because none of you did, and anyway we thought we weren't at the bridge yet.'

Jo swallowed the words *Why on earth didn't you shout out?* It wasn't Scott's fault they were lost. 'How far back?'

Scott thought about it. 'Ages ago. Before you stopped last time.'

'So what now? You reckon we're somewhere up here?' Jo pointed towards the top-left corner, where Nathan had indicated the wrong stream.

'No,' Nathan said. 'This map's only the orienteering course and a bit off the edges. Not the whole area. We're right off the map.'

Slowly, Jo looked around, at the featureless moorland and the sweeping rain. They were lost, out of the area they were supposed to keep to, off the map, with no compass, in a mist: and no one knew where they were. They could hardly have failed more spectacularly. Unless they were still out here by the time it got dark.

And, by now, that was a distinct possibility.

Presentations

She tried not to panic.

But her imagination wouldn't be held in check. She thought of Mountain Rescue being called out, teams of searchers working through the night. You could die of exposure, even in summer, Gary had said, and it was getting cold now. It would get dark early, because of the low cloud.

'What we should do now,' Nathan said, 'is sit by that big rock over there and have something to eat and drink.'

Jo told herself not to be ridiculous. They were only a matter of a few miles from the Centre. They wouldn't die of exposure. The worst thing they had to face was the disgrace of being incompetent, being a nuisance and coming last in the competition. Nathan was quite right: if people started getting cold and hungry and tired, it wouldn't help. Food was important. And part of the reason for sitting down by the rock was to consider their situation calmly and work out what to do.

They ate their chocolate and nuts, and Jo shared out the Kendal Mint Cake which Gary had said should be saved for an emergency. Well, this *was* an emergency. Opinion was divided between going back the way they had come (Hayley and Scott) and trying to find a direction which would take them back to the Centre (Jo and Nathan). 'It isn't as if we *can* go back the way we came,' Jo pointed out, 'now that we've wandered so far from the stream we came up. We might end up going down a different stream altogether and getting even more lost.'

'We know which way *not* to go.' Nathan lifted his juice carton in the direction of the hillside behind the boulder.

'That's right. If we went up higher, we'd end up in the middle of the Black Mountains,' Jo agreed. 'And we know the hostel's vaguely in this direction.' She waved to her left. 'So if we skirt round, then start going down when we see a stream, we *ought* to end up somewhere near the bridge.'

'I'm cold,' Hayley moaned. 'And my feet are wet. These boots are useless.'

Jo saw that Scott was shivering, too. His gloves were only woollen ones, soaked and useless, with the sleeves of his waterproof not long enough to cover them. The panicky feeling surged up again as Jo wondered how long it took for people to succumb to exposure. What would she do if Hayley sat there and refused to move?

'Come on, let's get going,' she said.

Then Nathan remembered something else. 'The whistle. Who's got the whistle?'

Jo clapped her hand to her waterproof pocket. 'I have. I forgot all about it.'

'Give a good blast on it then. Six blasts, like Gary said. I bet someone's out looking for us by now.'

Jo found the whistle in her pocket – thankfully she hadn't managed to pull it out earlier by mistake, and lose it. She felt shaken by the realisation of how useless she was. And she'd been so conceited at the beginning! – fancying that she was the only one capable of getting the team organised. It had been Nathan who realised how badly they'd wandered off course, while she hadn't even had the sense to think of using the whistle. Left to her, they'd still be trudging up into the Black Mountains. She held the whistle to her mouth with shaking fingers and blew six blasts, then listened. Nothing in reply.

'Give it a few more,' Nathan said.

It was too cold to stay still for long. They had to keep moving, or they'd really be in trouble. Nathan led the way, following a sheep path that countoured round the shoulder of hill, but Jo felt too crushed to have any faith at all in the direction they were taking. Plod, plod, her feet tramped on, swishing the stiff grass, sinking into the waterlogged peat. She kept turning her head to make sure Hayley and Scott were close behind. The four of them were enclosed in their own private world – a bowl of cloud, with nothing around but oozing water, bog grass, dim grey light, lashing rain. They could walk on like this until it got dark, and then what? The normal world of houses and people and mealtimes had faded to irrelevance, quite out of reach.

'Try that whistle again,' Nathan said, after what seemed a very long while.

Six blasts. They sounded caught and trapped in the mist, bouncing back like an echo off a cave wall. No one could possibly hear except nearby sheep. Jo heard the cry of some mountain bird, high and mournful.

Nathan grabbed her arm. 'Someone's whistling back. Keep going.'

Jo blew again as loudly as she could, though she knew Nathan was mistaken and it was only some bird blundering towards them. But—

'Yesss!' Hayley clenched both fists high in the air.

'Shh – listen again—'

'Didn't you hear? Three whistle blasts, over there!'

They all peered into the gloom as if willing some genie to materialise, some marsh spirit or will-o'-the-wisp.

'Over here!' Nathan shouted, waving his arms like someone signalling a helicopter to land.

And then the whistle sounded again, much closer. Three blobs of colour: blue, scarlet, blue. Three looming figures, not spectral or wisp-like but wonderfully solid and normal; concerned faces beneath pulled-down hoods. Mr Kershaw, Imogen and Gary.

'—And the booby prize, the Headless Chicken Award for not only failing to complete the course but for wandering right off it, goes to Hayley, Scott, Jo and Nathan,' Steve Kershaw announced.

Cheers, boos and catcalls. Jo made her way with the others towards Steve, and received a Cadbury's Creme Egg as her prize.

'Don't eat it all at once,' Steve warned. Nathan made a flamboyant bow as he accepted his egg, and Scott looked as pleased as if he'd really done something spectacular. The winners of the real prize, Natalie and her team, were already splitting open their big Easter egg and sharing out the contents.

'Give you some lessons in compass-work, Jo?' Natalie called out as Jo went back to her place.

It was their last night at Penhowell. The barbecue

had had to take place indoors, because of the weather, and after everything had been cleared away there was going to be a disco. When Steve had made some final announcements about clearing rooms in the morning, someone tapped Jo on the shoulder and she turned to find herself looking into Mrs Hughes' weathered face.

'A moment, Jo. I'd like a word with you, please. And Lynette. Can you both round up all the others from your room, and bring them to the office?'

'What's this all about?' Jo asked Lynette in an undertone, as they made their way.

Lynette looked at her scathingly. 'What do you think?'

Mrs Hughes didn't leave them in any doubt for long. In her no-nonsense manner, she told them, 'I want to know about the drinking last night. Who had what, who drank it and where it came from.'

There was an awkward silence. Ellie looked studiously at the ground; Lynette opened her mouth, but no sound came out; Natalie gazed at the ceiling; Hayley, rashly, giggled. Mrs Hughes silenced her with a glare.

'I don't find it amusing. And don't try to waste any more of my time. Did all of you drink alcohol last night?'

'No,' Jo said. 'Ellie and Lynette didn't have any.'

'But you did?'

'Yes.'

Mrs Hughes held her glance for a moment, and then said, 'Ellie and Lynette, you can go.'

Ellie, looking most uncomfortable, darted a look at Jo and went out. Lynette paused in the doorway. 'But Jo only—'

'Leave it to me, please.' Somehow, Mrs Hughes could make a soft, silky voice sound more threatening than a shout. 'No doubt Jo can tell me about it herself.'

Lynette mouthed, 'Tell her,' at Jo, behind Mrs Hughes' back, and closed the door.

'Well? Who brought the stuff? Where did it come from?' Mrs Hughes demanded. And then, when no one spoke, 'Come on. I don't plan to stand here all evening.'

The door opened and Steve Kershaw came in. For some reason, this made it worse – Jo wasn't used to being lumped together with Natalie as partner-in-crime – but, remembering that Mr Kershaw had failings of his own, she met his eye defiantly.

'I asked who brought the stuff,' Mrs Hughes repeated.

Hayley looked at Natalie; Natalie said nothing, but that was enough.

'Natalie? You did, I take it?'

'Why are you picking on me?' Natalie's voice rose harshly. 'It's always the same, isn't it? Always me that gets into trouble!'

'You do seem to have rather a knack, yes. Did you bring the stuff or not?'

Leanne rubbed the worn carpet with her toe. 'Say yes, Nat,' she mumbled.

Natalie gave her a look of loathing. 'All right then, I did! But we all drank it.'

'And how much was there, exactly?' Mrs Hughes was looking at Hayley now.

'Can't remember,' Hayley muttered. 'Some vodka and some whisky.'

'Right. That's what I found in the cupboard in your room.' Mrs Hughes reached for a carrier bag on the floor and pulled out the two empty bottles. 'So these were yours, Natalie? Where did you get them?'

Natalie, wearing an expression of intense boredom, picked at a fingernail. 'I had the whisky in my bag. I bought the vodka the other day in town.'

'Really.' Mrs Hughes' voice was cutting. 'We give you an hour to yourselves and you use it to break the law by buying spirits.'

'That's the shop's fault, isn't it? They didn't ask my age.'

'You knew perfectly well what you were doing. And breaking the school rules is *your* fault.' Her glance swept over the four of them. 'So, last night you decided to get drunk?'

No one answered.

'Leanne? Hayley? Jo? You all had some?'

Leanne and Hayley nodded. Mrs Hughes swivelled round to stare at Jo. Jo hesitated, weighing up her options. What would be worse? Allow herself to be lumped together with the others? Or tell the truth, keep herself out of serious trouble, but have Natalie out to get her?

She nodded. Mrs Hughes looked at her in disappointment. Then Leanne said, 'She only had one tiny sip of vodka. Just to taste.'

Natalie's eyes rolled upwards. Mrs Hughes said, 'Is that right, Jo?'

'Yes.'

'You're sure? Just one taste?'

'Yes.'

'But the rest of you put away this lot.' Mrs Hughes was still holding the bottles, one in each hand. 'No wonder you were sick this morning,' she said scathingly to Hayley.

Mr Kershaw, who had been leaning against the desk saying nothing, now launched in. 'I hope you realise how irresponsible you've been? How serious this is?' His eyes, hard and angry, met each girl's in turn. 'I'm going to have to report this to the Head, back at school. I can't overlook it. And that will probably mean parents being brought in.' He turned away with a gesture of exasperation. 'Do you realise how much work goes into organising a week like this? How careful we have to be about safety? How much responsibility the staff have to take? No, I'm sure you don't. You're too concerned with what silly little games you can get up to in your room, and whether you can get one past us.' He glared at Hayley. 'We're not stupid. If someone looks like she has a hangover and throws up, it does tend to make us just a weeny bit suspicious. What were you trying to prove, for Pete's sake? And going out in mountain terrain so boozed-up that you can't even keep hold of a compass and end up getting your whole team lost – it's moronic! Hasn't anything we've dinned into you about safety, even one word of it, actually sunk in?'

Hayley, red-faced and blinking back tears, said nothing. Turning to Natalie, Mr Kershaw went on, 'So you were the one who actually bought the stuff, were you? Brilliant! Should we search your bag to see what else might be in there?'

'There isn't anything,' Natalie muttered. Jo wondered whether Mr Kershaw knew about the cigarettes, and how much worse it would make things if he did.

Mr Kershaw looked sceptically at Natalie. 'How

can I believe what you say? You've proved yourself totally unreliable. Jo – you can go, since you weren't so much involved as the others.' He didn't look at her, indicating the door with a twist of his head. 'The rest of you—'

Jo went out and closed the door behind her, hearing Mr Kershaw's voice rise in a renewed tirade. She had never seen him so angry before, and if she had really been as much to blame as the other three she would have been seriously ashamed of herself. As it was, her legs were shaking and her stomach churning more than when she'd been halfway up a rock face. If it hadn't been for Leanne, she'd still be in there.

She could still feel her cheeks burning as she went outside into the drizzle. She didn't feel able to face Lynette and Ellie, just yet. The disco music had started, the tables had been cleared and through the window Jo could see Lynette dancing with Damien. Jo didn't feel like dancing. She turned to face the dark rise of the hillside and breathed in the damp, clean air. Tomorrow night she'd be back at home with Mum and Nan, and this would seem like something that had happened ages ago.

'Jo?'

She turned, and saw Ellie behind her, wearing her kagoule.

'I thought I saw you come out. Are you OK?'

Jo smiled. 'Yes, thanks.'

'Did they have a real go at you?'

'Yes. The others are still in there. Leanne told them I'd only had a taste, and he let me come out. Not a very nice end to the course. But it was a fair cop.' Jo didn't want to talk about it. She looked at Ellie, whose face was almost concealed by the hood of her waterproof and by her springy hair, dampened and shining with raindrops.

'Have you enjoyed it, this week?' Jo asked. There had been times when she'd wondered.

'Oh, yes!' Ellie said. 'It's been great. The mountains and the waterfalls, and doing things that scared me stiff.' She hesitated. 'Sharing the room – that was the worst bit. But even that wasn't as bad as I thought.'

'People like Natalie,' Jo said, 'well – they're not going to change, are they? So you just have to get along with them as best you can.'

Ellie stretched out a hand to the soft rain. 'What amazes me is how she gets away with things. Doesn't she?'

'Not with this. She'll be in worse trouble than anyone else, because she was the one who bought the booze.'

'Yes, but what'll happen? Her mum will be brought in and Natalie'll get another telling-off and a warning from the Head. It won't bother her. She'll carry on exactly as she is.'

'I suppose so. Unless she gets suspended.'

'Even that wouldn't worry her. She'd find another school and start all over again.' Ellie sighed. 'But there are some things she shouldn't be allowed to get away with.'

'Oh, you mean that Mr Wishart business last term?'

Ellie nodded. 'That was much worse than this. I still think about him sometimes, and wonder if he's got another job.'

'Do you? He'd be pleased if he knew.'

'Come on.' Suddenly Ellie looked embarrassed. 'You haven't got your coat on. Let's go back in.'

Crossing the border back into England next morning felt like leaving a whole chunk of experience behind. Jo stared at the main-road traffic, already feeling a tug of nostalgia for slate villages, hazy summits and road signs in Welsh. There had been let-downs along with the pleasures: Mr Kershaw's affair, her own incompetence yesterday, the telling-off. But there had been more than enough to compensate. Jo felt like an addict, yearning for the next fix. When?

And Mr Kershaw had been right, teamwork was one of the most important things to learn. Out there yesterday, until they were rescued, the four of them *had* been a team, even if a grudging and hopeless one. They had depended on each other, for those brief intense hours.

Nathan. Jo could see him ahead of her, next to Sanjay, staring moodily out of the window, his fingers shredding a sweet wrapper. He'd been quite different yesterday: positive, capable. He had spoken to her intelligibly, instead of in mumbles and grunts. He'd even *smiled*. Jo wondered whether he'd go back to being the same difficult, surly boy in the classroom next term. Even if so, she knew a different Nathan now.

They weren't going straight back to school. The coach stopped at Symond's Yat, just over the border, for a final walk down steep woodland to the River Wye. When they returned, they went up to a railed promontory overlooking the loops and bends of the river. You could sometimes see peregrine falcons from here, Mrs Hughes explained.

'While we're all together, for the last time,' Mr Kershaw announced when they were all back at the coach, 'there are some final presentations to make. First, I'm not sure whether Mrs Hughes knows we know this, but it's her birthday today. We won't embarrass her by saying *which* birthday it is, but—' He delved under one of the front seats and brought out a cardboard box, whipping off the lid with a conjuror's flourish to reveal a huge iced cake. 'And here's one I prepared earlier...no, seriously, the woman at the pub in Penhowell does cake-decoration in a big way, so Miss Kelland and I sneaked off there one night to order this.' He tilted the cake so that everyone could see the red dragon that sprawled across the iced surface, and then produced a box of matches from his pocket. 'Only one candle to blow out, Olwen, and then you can cut it up...'

Joining in the chorus of '*Happy Birthday to You*', Jo caught Lynette's eye and smiled.

'I told you!' Lynette mouthed at her.

Jo didn't mind having been completely mistaken. The pub visit was explained: Mr Kershaw's image could remain intact, and Miss Kelland could leave school without a blemish on her character.

'Second, as you know, Miss Kelland's leaving school today,' Mr Kershaw went on. 'I'd like to thank her for all her support this week, and for coping with you lot. And wish her all the best for her new job. Also, she probably won't mind me mentioning that she's getting married—'

'I *told* you there was nothing in it!' Lynette whispered. 'Her and Mr Kershaw – whose stupid idea was that?'

Now, there was only the last boring bit of the journey home, watching the scenery flatten into regular, fenced fields, cut up by dual carriageways and road works. The coach's progress was punctuated by Little Chefs and garden centres at regular intervals. Where are the mountains? Jo wanted to demand of someone. Where are the wild bits? It looked so flat and tame. She had left part of herself behind in Wales.

Back at school, in the late afternoon, there were clusters of parents waiting. Among them was Mr Kershaw's wife, smiling and waving, with the baby in a pushchair: Steve leaped down from the coach and gave her a bear hug, and then he scooped up the baby boy and lifted him high. Jo smiled, looking round for Mum as she climbed stiffly down.

Dad was there, with Helen.

'Hi there, love.' He came over and kissed her.

'But I thought Mum—'

'She asked me to come instead. She's gone away.'

Gone Away

'Gone away?' Jo echoed. 'Gone where?'

She imagined Mum packing up and setting off in despair, all her possessions stuffed into her car. Giving up, running away. Where to? Where *could* she run to? Jo *knew* she should have done something sooner. It was her fault. She shouldn't have gone and left Mum in her depressed state.

'Only for the weekend,' Dad said. 'She's gone to see that friend of hers, in Ilkley, I think she said. Yorkshire. Sonia, or Sylvia, whatever her name is. You know the one I mean.'

'You mean Stella? Mum's friend Stella?'

'That's the one.'

Dad ought to remember. Stella had been Mum's best friend, after all, till she'd moved away; she used to drop in to see Mum quite often – back in the other life, when they'd been a family, and lived in the old house. Stella and Mum had once worked together in the same insurance office, and though they'd both left ages ago they'd stayed friends. Stella's marriage had broken up a few years ago, Jo remembered. Stella and Mum had that in common now.

'But what about the shop?' Jo asked. 'You mean Mum's cleared off and left the shop closed?' It didn't look hopeful.

'I think she needed a break,' Dad said. 'Let's get your bag.'

The coach driver was pulling bags out from the hold with a long hooked pole. Jo recognised hers and went to fetch it. She felt abandoned. Mum had cleared off without even telling her. She wanted to go home, not to Dad's house.

'Here, let me carry it,' Helen said, darting over.

'It's all right. I can manage.' Jo heaved her bag away from the others. Trust Dad to bring Helen here, for everyone to see her – several people knew she wasn't Jo's mum. In any case, Helen looked too young to be the mother of anyone in Year Nine. She was eye-catchingly dressed in a long red sweater and black trousers, with her hair tied back. Her smile struck Jo as self-conscious, knowing people were looking at her. Jo felt no sympathy; Helen hadn't needed to come.

'Bye, Jo. Have a good holiday.' That was Natalie, coming over for the sole purpose, Jo was well aware, of getting a good look at Helen. New gossip fodder.

'There's Lynette,' Dad said, as Lynette came over to say goodbye. 'Lynette, why don't you come over this weekend to see Jo? She'll be over at my place. You two haven't met, have you?' he said to Helen. 'Lyn, this is Helen.' His voice was loud enough to be heard by anyone who hadn't already realised that he had a new and younger woman in tow.

Jo dropped her bag and went over to Mr Kershaw, who was supervising luggage collection at the back of the coach.

'Thanks, Mr Kershaw,' she said. 'It's been great.' And suddenly she felt like crying.

Mr Kershaw turned round and looked at her, and then Dad came up behind her, smiling.

'Hello there,' he said in the jovial way that Jo found so embarrassing. 'Richard Cannon – we've met before. Thanks for organising all this – rather you than me!'

Mr Kershaw shook the hand Dad was holding out (why did Dad have to *do* that, as if they were at a business meeting?) and Dad went on, 'I hope she's behaved herself.' He tousled Jo's hair as if she were a three-year-old, or a dog.

For a heart-stopping moment Jo wondered whether Mr Kershaw was going to tell Dad about her misdemeanours and failings: leaving the Centre without permission, drinking alcohol, getting her team hopelessly lost on the orienteering course.

But of course he didn't. He said, 'I think you've had a great time, haven't you, Cannonball? It's right up your street.'

Good old Steve. She should have known he wouldn't let her down.

Jo *had* to talk to Dad about Mum. This weekend, before Mum got any more desperate.

She'd been trying to forget about Helen, wishing she'd melted away during the last week, leaving Dad lonely and available for Mum. But Helen was all too obviously still in the picture, with Dad parading her about. Helen, glossy and sleek, somehow had an air of success about her, like a thoroughbred racehorse being led into the winner's enclosure to be photographed and garlanded with flowers. *She* wouldn't start up a business that was doomed to failure and then let herself get depressed. No, she was an interior designer, the sort of person who'd end up featured in glossy magazines, with famous people pursuing her to do up their houses.

In the car, Helen sat sideways to ask Jo all sorts of questions about the week away. She was far more interested than Dad, really, and so friendly that it took an effort for Jo to see her as an encumbrance, a rival for Mum who would have to be got rid of. Jo hoped Dad would drop Helen off at her own flat on the way home, but he didn't; Helen was obviously coming with them. And, even worse, when Jo went up to the bathroom, she found definite signs of occupation in there: deodorant and shampoo and shower gel, with names like *Wild Musk* and *Orchid Essence* that showed they weren't Dad's. An extra toothbrush in the holder. Tissues in a pretty flowered box. Things weren't looking good.

Jo sneaked a look into Dad's bedroom. The bed was neatly made, with two cushions arranged on the duvet. Jo's heart sank further. This was decisive proof. Dad *never* made his bed; he always left the duvet in a rumpled heap. Helen had moved in.

Poor Mum. Had anyone told her?

Jo couldn't even remember her script for the conversation she was going to have with Dad. She tried out a new version:

Jo: *Helen, I know you've only just moved in, but the fact is it's a bit inconvenient. Could you possibly move out again? Mum and I want Dad for ourselves.*

Helen (obligingly): *Yes, fine. How soon do you want him?*

Why didn't she face it? She was no good as a scriptwriter. But she still had to find a way of helping Mum. And she couldn't confront Dad on the subject with Helen around.

She tried dropping hints. With Helen busy in the kitchen, Jo collared Dad in the lounge. 'Are you doing anything special this weekend, Dad? Is Helen going to be here tomorrow?'

Dad cleared his throat. 'Er...well. The thing is, Helen lives here now. So yes, she will be around. Oh, and by the way there's a party we've got to go to tomorrow night. I nearly forgot. Not the sort of thing I could take you to, really. You could have Lynette round if you like.'

Great. Jo tried not to mind – after all, Dad and Helen hadn't expected her to be here this weekend.

'Helen's cooking for us tonight,' Dad said. 'She's a great cook.'

By now there were several hefty obstacles in the path of Jo's plan, but she clung to the idea that Dad would still help somehow. However besotted he might be with Helen, he still wouldn't want Mum's business to collapse, if it was in his power to save it. How much money would it take? Hundreds of pounds, thousands? How much could Dad afford? Jo had no idea.

She couldn't raise the subject in front of Helen.

Helen might sympathise, and Jo didn't want Helen showing pity for Mum. It would be rubbing in the fact that Helen was a winner and Mum was a loser.

Delicious smells were wafting from the kitchen. No doubt Dad was right, and Helen was a brilliant cook as well as everything else. It didn't seem right that Helen should excel at something Jo thought of as Mum's domain. Mum was the cook in the family, though Dad had never shown as much appreciation of Mum's efforts as he apparently did of Helen's.

'Not lentil stew again,' he used to say. 'Can't we have a decent steak?'

Helen probably cooked him steak. Perhaps steak was what she was cooking now. Jo's stomach turned over at the thought of meat. She had always had the vegetarian choices at Penhowell, and hadn't eaten red meat for so long that she might as well be a proper vegetarian, like Mum.

It wasn't easy to get Dad on his own. Jo prepared her first sentence, and rehearsed it so well that it almost kept popping out of her mouth all on its own, but Dad kept hovering around Helen in the kitchen: linking his arms round her waist from behind, lifting saucepan lids, chopping parsley. At last Helen sent him out to the dustbin with a bag of scraps. (Jo noticed several things in the bag which Mum would have recycled – a bottle, stuff for the compost heap, a tin can – but didn't feel like launching into a lecture on environmental responsibility and conservation of the world's resources.) She seized her chance, following Dad out to the twilit garden.

It was a mild spring evening. Dad's one tree was coming into leaf and a blackbird was singing from its branches. There were a few daffodils in a tub on the patio and some low evergreen shrubs, but apart from that the garden waited for attention.

'It's not much of a garden yet,' Dad said, coming round the corner from the dustbin.

Jo waited for the inevitable next remark, and it came.

'Helen will soon sort it out. She loves gardening.'

Jo tried not to grit her teeth. 'Good.'

Dad came and stood beside Jo and put an arm across her shoulders. 'You don't mind, do you? About Helen moving in?'

'It doesn't make much difference whether I mind or not, does it?' Jo said ungraciously. 'She's here now.'

'Come on, Jo.' Dad pulled her closer, almost getting her in a headlock.

She wriggled free. 'Listen, Dad. You've got to help.'

This was it. Suddenly her mouth was dry, her rehearsals useless. She'd forgotten her own lines, let alone Dad's.

'Help with what?' he asked. 'Was there some

problem, last week? I *thought* you were quiet.'

'No, it's not that. The week was great. I'm really glad you paid for me to go. No, it's Mum. Her shop's not making money and she's getting really depressed about it.'

'I know that.' Dad let go of her. 'But I don't see what I can do to help.'

'Of course you can help! It only needs some more money. You've got to spend money to make money – that's what you said. You could lend her some, couldn't you?'

'It's not as simple as that.' Dad was frowning into the dusk. 'The other saying that comes to mind is *There's no point throwing good money after bad.* The only thing that would save that shop is uprooting it and planting it in the middle of Milton Keynes. And even then there'd be no guarantee. I mean, health shops are hardly big crowd-pullers, are they? You've got to admit that.'

'So what are you saying, then?' Jo tried to stay calm. 'That Mum might as well give up?'

'Yes, really. Either cut her losses and give up now, or put a lot more effort into it and face a lot more disappointment.'

'But what would she do, if she does give up? How's she going to earn money? Running that shop is all she *wants* to do.'

'We've got to be realistic, Jo. If the shop can't support itself, it's no use pretending it can. I've said all along – I told Steff – that she'd be far better off getting herself a decent office job, a full-time one. A guaranteed salary every month could have saved her all this worry. If she'd stayed at the insurance office, she could have done all right. Whether she can get back there now, I don't know – she could have gone to evening classes to improve her qualifications—'

'Mum does go to an evening class,' Jo said. 'A literature class. She reads all these books all the time about poets and Frankenstein and stuff.'

Dad puffed up his cheeks and blew out the air. 'Yes, and what good's that going to do her? What use is knowing about literature? In the real world, I mean?'

'So you won't help?' Jo said flatly.

'If there was something I could do, reasonably and practically, I would. Obviously I don't want your Mum to end up on the dole, and I'm not going to see either of you go without things you need. But I can't save that shop. I don't know how much money you think I've got, anyway. I've spent a lot on this house, and then there's the new car...'

'Supper's nearly ready,' Helen called brightly, appearing at the patio doors. 'What are you two doing, out here in the dark? I've poured the

Chardonnay, Rich, and isn't anyone going to lay the table for me?'

Jo almost hated her.

There seemed to be some problem about when Jo was going home. She had assumed Dad would drive her back on Sunday night, but now it seemed that Mum wouldn't be coming home till Monday or Tuesday.

'Nan's there,' Jo pointed out.

'No, apparently she's gone off on some walking trip.'

'What, *another* one?'

Did neither of them have any sense of responsibility? Mum and Nan, both of them, taking off when it suited them? Jo couldn't entirely dispel the thought that maybe Mum had gone for good; maybe she wasn't coming back at all. Going to Stella's, Jo thought, would only be likely to cast Mum even deeper into gloom: Stella's craft shop seemed to be thriving, according to the exuberant postcards which arrived every so often.

Jo spent Saturday evening at Lynette's. Lynette's mum made one of her special throw-everything-in fruit curries, stirring the ingredients into a huge saucepan; the two girls helped with the peeling and chopping. On the packet of cumin seed, Jo saw the green *Harvest* label, and the price written in her own handwriting.

'Oh! You've been to Mum's shop!' she exclaimed.

'That's right. Went there last Saturday,' Lynette's mum said. 'Best health-food shop for miles around. You tell your mum that.'

There were two health-food shops in Hagley Heath, and it was a ten mile round trip to Beckley. Lynette was deliberately nonchalant as she chopped green chillies; then she gave a quick, furtive glance at Jo, saw Jo looking, and smiled. Lynette, obviously, had sent her mum; only problem was, Jo thought, that it would take another hundred or so Lynette's mums to save *Harvest*.

Lynette rounded up Gavin and Gary from their football game outside, sent them firmly to wash their hands, then herded them to the table. 'And *don't* squirt lemon slices at each other, like last time we had curry!'

The meal was eaten to the accompaniment of *The Magic Flute*, the latest in Lynette's dad's repertoire. At first he was quiet, listening intently, eating in slow motion.

'Wait for it,' Lynette warned Jo in a stage whisper. 'He's working up to a performance.'

'Please, not *Queen of the Night* again,' begged her mother. 'We've had this every day this week. I had to sew a new button on his trousers yesterday.'

Lynette's dad slowly put down his knife and fork. Then, striking a dramatic pose, he joined in with the soprano in a strangulated voice, lifting himself right out of his chair and pulling anguished faces as he strained for the highest notes, which were *very* high. The boys bounced and clapped, smiling their identical broad smiles. Lynette winced and clapped her hands over her ears. Her mum rolled up a paper napkin and lobbed it at him. 'Is someone murdering a cat? Be quiet and eat your dinner, you great wailing warbler!'

'Forgot to tell you it's Karaoke night.'

'Karaoke night?' Her mum raised an eyebrow. 'More like strangle-a-parrot night, with this DIY diva in the house.'

Jo gave a snorting laugh that dissolved into giggles, then caught Lynette's eye and set her off too. Lynette started to choke on a piece of popadum; Gavin shoved his chair aside and thumped her on the back; their mother threw up her hands and fetched a glass of water from the kitchen. All the time their father continued to sing, spreading a hand against his chest, making big eyes and fluttering his lashes melodramatically. In the middle of laughing, Jo felt a deep tug of sadness. Ages ago, they used to fool around like this – Jo, her mum, her dad.

*

On Sunday, Dad and Helen had friends for lunch, people called Jeremy and Ingrid who had very loud voices and treated Jo as if she were ten, when they bothered to take any notice of her at all. Most of the time she might as well have been invisible. Helen cooked again, very impressively, but the meal wasn't nearly as much fun as the curry at Lynette's last night. Jo couldn't help noticing that Helen behaved differently in front of the guests: speaking in a way Jo thought of as affected, putting on a sophisticated act. Dad kept putting his arm round Helen and holding her hand and generally behaving as if they were Siamese twins, finishing remarks with '...don't we, love?' He didn't act like that when was alone with Helen and Jo, and Jo didn't like it now. He was like someone showing off a new possession.

She wanted to go home. Her mood wasn't helped on Sunday night when the phone rang and she heard Dad talking, obviously to Mum. 'Yes, fine. Tuesday, then. No problem.'

'Didn't she want to talk to me?' Jo asked when he rang off.

'I think she was in a hurry,' Dad said. 'She's decided to stay up there an extra day, and drive back tomorrow evening. I'll run you back home on Tuesday. Not that there's any problem if you wanted to stay here all week. Helen and I are going out on

Wednesday night and then we'll be away for the Easter weekend, but—'

Gloomily, Jo pictured her future as a semi-orphan, shuttling between Dad and Helen, and Mum and Nan, when they hadn't got anything more important to do.

Outward Bound

'So Dad didn't give you my message, then?' Mum said on Tuesday in the shop.

'What message? All he said was you were staying an extra day with Stella and he was bringing me back this morning.'

'Oh, he is *useless* sometimes! I told him to make sure to tell you I had news for you, but I was keeping it till I saw you.'

Jo looked at her suspiciously. The shop was quiet, as usual – a lone customer, a young woman with a small child in a buggy, was sorting through the packets of nuts. Mum, far from looking haggard and disillusioned as Jo had expected, was looking fresh and pretty in her mauve jumper, a new string of beads and even make-up. She looked as if she'd had a real holiday, not just three days away.

'What news?' Jo asked, cautiously.

Mum was fitting a new till-roll. 'The first is, Nan's

going to move out. I know you'll say something sarcastic – she's getting married!'

'*Married?* What, at her age?'

Mum smiled. 'That's just what I knew you'd say. Yes, at her age. You may not have noticed, but even at her age she's been having a very interesting time lately. I suppose you think she should be moving into an old people's home and taking up bingo – but no, she's getting married.'

'To Dennis?'

Mum laughed. 'Yes, of course to Dennis, unless there've been other developments while I've been away!'

Jo tidied the rack of muesli bars near the till. Well, good for Nan, she thought; Dennis was quite nice, but it didn't strike Jo as the right sort of thing to be happening. If anyone was going to meet a new man and get married, it ought to be Mum.

'And you'll never guess what they're doing for their honeymoon?'

'I don't know. Going to Brighton? Blackpool? No, probably going on some Ramblers' holiday.'

'You're getting closer. They're going trekking in Nepal. In the Himalayas.'

'Wow! *Nan* is?'

'She's always wanted to do it, and Dennis has been there before. They booked it up as soon as they decided to get married.'

'When's the wedding?'

'Oh, soon,' Mum said. 'There's no point hanging around, at their age – oh, you've got me saying it now! And they're going to move into Dennis' house, in Daventry.'

Jo decided that if *she* ever got married – not that she thought it at all likely – she was going trekking in Nepal for her honeymoon. So, Nan was moving out – but there was more, she could tell. Mum had that look of bursting to say something.

'What else has happened?' she asked. 'Why did you spend so long at Stella's? Leaving the shop closed again?'

The woman with the baby approached the till, paid for one packet of pistachio nuts and went out, leaving the shop empty.

'I've been doing some serious thinking,' Mum said, lowering her voice even though there was no one to hear. 'And I've made some decisions. For both of us.'

'Oh.' Jo looked down at the pricelist of Mum's home-made produce that was taped to the desk, and realised that there was no home-made stuff on sale today because Mum hadn't done any cooking. 'I know what you're going to say. You've decided to close the shop, haven't you?'

'Yes. It's not working, we both know that.'

This was where Jo had planned to make her announcement...

> Jo: (smugly) *No, it's all taken care of. Dad's going to give you ten thousand pounds.* (She had always been a bit vague about the sum of money needed, but felt that ten thousand pounds ought to cover it.)

> Mum: (surprised but radiant) *Oh, Richard is so wonderful! I must thank him in person...*

...if it hadn't been for the small snags that Dad wouldn't play, being so wrapped up in Helen, and Mum obviously had plans of her own. Mentally, Jo consigned her script to the waste-paper bin.

'What do you mean?' she asked. 'Are you going to look for another job?'

Mum smiled, uncertainly. 'I think I've already got one. Jo, how do you like the idea of moving to Yorkshire?'

'Moving? But we've only just moved here! And *Yorkshire*?'

'Yes. But this would be a complete move. A new start for both of us. Leaving the shop. Leaving your school.' Mum hesitated, twisting the string of beads round and round her little finger. 'Living farther away from Dad.'

'What's happened, then? Have you found a job in Yorkshire?'

'You know Stella runs a craft shop? Well, she's doing well – it's in Ilkley, you know, a lovely country town but with tourists all year round. You'd love it, Jo – it's in the Yorkshire Dales, with the hills and moors on the doorstep. Stella and I went to Haworth, where the Brontës lived – that's not far away. Wuthering Heights country...'

'You're going to move in with Stella?' Jo wasn't at all sure how good an idea this could be. Sharing, in her experience, caused difficulties, even with people you liked. 'Work in her craft shop?'

'No, no. There's a little tea shop next door and the people who own it are selling up – retiring. Stella's been thinking of expanding – business has been so good – and she was thinking of buying the place next door as a sort of gallery extension. But when I told her about my problems, she said why not keep it as a tea shop? She can still display paintings and pottery there for sale and I can run it as a wholefood café, with light lunches and teas—'

Mum was completely sold on the idea, Jo could tell. But then Mum had been just as enthusiastic about *this* shop. If this new idea only led to more disappointment, then what? Jo thought of all the things Dad had said and wondered how many of them were true.

'It's all set up, with a lovely little kitchen. I could sell food to take away as well. And best of all, I won't be on my own any more. We'll be partners. Stella and Steff!' Suddenly, noticing Jo's silence, Mum stopped and looked at her doubtfully. 'What do you think? I know it'd be a wrench for you, leaving school, but at least you'd be able to start a new school at the beginning of your exam courses. I stayed on an extra day to go to estate agents about renting a flat and I even went and had a look at the school – they do the Duke of Edinburgh Award there, so you could do all your outdoor stuff, go on trips to places like the Peak District and the Lakes. And you could have Lynette to stay, I know you'd miss her—'

'Hang on a minute, Mum! Is this all settled?' Jo felt as if the rug underneath her feet had whisked itself into the air and turned itself into a flying carpet, whooshing her away from her normal life altogether.

'Sorry, I haven't given you a chance to say anything. Well, what do you think? Do you think it's a good idea?'

'Does Dad know?'

'No. He doesn't.' Mum seemed to shrink back a little into her old self. 'I know what he'd say – *Don't throw good money after bad.* I *know* there's no guarantee this will work, no way of taking out an insurance policy. But I've thought about it carefully and so has Stella, and we both think there's more chance of succeeding there than here.'

'He'd probably say you should get a job like the one you used to have, in an office,' Jo said cautiously.

'Yes, I know he would. But I don't want his advice, Jo. I don't want to play safe and work nine to five in an office. I want to use my own initiative – do something that interests me. There's something else we'll have to discuss,' Mum said, a bit reluctantly. 'The three of us.'

'What?' Jo asked. She thought, there are four of us now. Dad and Helen, Mum and me. Two separate families, not one.

'Well – I mean—' Mum started fiddling with the price label gun. 'I've sort of assumed that you'd come with me, but we ought to discuss it. I mean, Dad might think you ought to live with him and only visit me in the holidays—'

'No,' Jo said quickly. 'Dad doesn't want that. I'm a bit in the way over at Dad's, to be honest. I want to come with you, Mum.' Lynette, she thought: I'll miss Lynette. That'll be the worst thing. She took a breath and said bravely, 'It sounds great.'

'Oh Jo, are you sure? You really don't mind?' Mum

looked giddy with relief. She didn't even mind when the next customer to enter the shop only asked the way to the post office and went out again without buying anything.

Jo remembered that she hadn't told Mum about the vodka-drinking incident or warned her that she might be called in to discuss it with the Head. There wasn't much point in mentioning it, just now; there were far more important things to talk about. Perhaps it would be quietly forgotten about over the Easter holidays.

Later, Jo went out on her mountain bike.

Soon, she thought, she'd be able to use it properly. She'd be able to go on long rides into the Yorkshire Dales and the North York Moors. Real wild country, not fenced and tamed fields like the ones surrounding her now. The East Midlands was putting on its best spring show, to make her feel guilty for preferring Wales and Yorkshire – the gardens were all foamed over with white and pink blossom, and the hedgerows full of cuckoo flowers and bluebells. The sun was warm on her back, making her think of tennis, reading in the garden, school sports day and long cool drinks. The coming summer term would be her last at Hagley Hall and then she would have to start all over again, meet new people and make new friends. She wasn't as confident about it as she had made herself sound, for Mum.

She needed time to get used to the idea.

She rode right over to the Country Park, left her bike at the shelter and ran to the top of one of the little conical hills. The landscape spread out in front of her, patches of fields and darker clumps of woodland, all frosted over with blossom. She could look back and see Beckley, the spire of the church and the town hall clock in the centre, and then, spreading outwards, the red rash of housing developments, the lorry park, the sweep of ring road, busy with traffic. Nearest of all, the big raw block that was *Toyz World*, with the sun reflecting off the roofs of cars in its car park. Dad would be in there, selling computer games and plastic toys, not knowing how glorious the spring day was, out in the sunshine.

In the other direction was landscape softening and fading to misty blues, and hills rising in the distance, all the way to the Welsh borders if only you could see. Mum was right to want to leave, Jo thought. They were hemmed in, in Beckley, restricted by things they couldn't control. And it wasn't good for Mum to live and work so close to Dad, where he could always see how bad business was, and tut at her, and tell her how she ought to have arranged things. Dad wouldn't really mind all that much, Jo thought, that they were going. He wouldn't care that she'd only be using her smart bedroom for holiday visits. He had Helen now.

There would be big changes ahead for all of them. Jo pictured Dad and Helen with a new baby, and Mum serving meals for friends in her cafe, laughing with Stella and drinking wine. It was time Mum enjoyed being a single woman, instead of letting her responsibilities weigh her down.

Changes. The prospect of such big changes could easily be alarming, if Jo let it. But she wasn't going to. She knew she could cope.

Now, she was going to cycle round to Lynette's and tell her all the news. That would be hard. Lynette was the best possible friend: understanding, loyal, fun to be with. They were used to seeing each other nearly every day, but after the summer they would only see each other in the holidays. Jo knew she would have to make the best of it, for Mum. She thought of Lynette coming to stay, of the two of them walking on the moors, and visiting Haworth where the Brontes had lived. They would stay friends, she was sure. Stella had e-mail, Mum had said; they could e-mail each other every day.

Suddenly she was impatient to see Lynette, and to talk about everything that was going to happen. She glanced around from her summit, then spread her arms out and ran down the slope as fast as she could, swooping and zigzagging, pretending to be an Olympic downhill skier doing the downhill slalom. In her imagination, the snow sprayed up on the turns, the edges of her skis dug in, she swivelled her hips and swooshed, daringly close to the poles. 'And Cannon's soaring into the lead,' an imaginary commentator enthused to the TV-watching millions. She reached the finishing poles, whooshed through and turned to accept the admiration of the crowd.

She grinned at herself, glad there was no one to see her, and then she thought *Why worry?* She didn't have to be mature and sensible *all* the time.

Linda Newbery
NO WAY BACK

Ellie and Amanda are best friends. Or they were, until Natalie arrived. Natalie is trouble from day one. And Ellie feels left out when Amanda starts going round with the new girl.

But then things start to go missing from the stables where Ellie works, and the finger of suspicion points at Natalie. When she makes a serious accusation against her new teacher, Ellie decides it's time to confront her.

Will Natalie back down? Will Ellie and Amanda make up and be friends again? Whatever happens there's no way back...

1 84121 582 1

£4.99

Linda Newbery
WINDFALL

Nathan is always in trouble. He doesn't want to be, it just seems to happen.

Then he finds Windfall, the local animal sanctuary, and things start to look up. He meets Saskia, the beautiful raven-haired girl who works there. And Hazel, a maltreated young dog nobody can get near to, except Nathan.

Nathan dreams of taking Hazel to live with his father. But how much time does Nathan's father have for him? And where can Nathan turn when everyone lets him down?

1 84121 586 4
£4.99

Brian Keaney

FALLING FOR JOSHUA

Abi had a strong desire to turn her head and look after him, just to remind herself what he looked like.

Abi knows there's something special about Josh the moment his deep blue eyes meet hers. But Abi has a secret. And she's so used to keeping it hidden that she just can't trust him. She's been rejected before, and she's no stranger to pain.

But one night something terrible happens and Abi's secret is revealed. Will Josh stand by her, and will Abi learn to accept the way she is?

'thoughtful and exciting'
Books for Keeps on
Brian Keaney's *Balloon House*

1 84121 858 8
£4.99

Andrew Matthews
WOLF SUMMER

'Anna? I'd like you to meet Pete.' Anna turned, and her breath was taken away. Pete was beautiful: black hair, an angular face with high cheekbones, dark brown eyes with sweeping lashes.

Pete's gorgeous. But unfriendly. And anyway, Anna's got other things on her mind. Sent away for the summer to stop her seeing her boyfriend, Anna is pining for her lost love.

But then she gets involved in the local wolf sanctuary, and discovers a thrilling and dangerous passion. A passion that eventually throws her and Pete together in a time of crisis.

A summer tale of love, longing, and wolves.

1 84121 758 1
£4.99

More Orchard Black Apples

Orchard Black Apples are available from all good bookshops,
or can be ordered direct from the publisher:
Orchard Books, PO BOX 29, Douglas IM99 1BQ
Credit card orders please telephone 01624 836000
or fax 01624 837033
or e-mail: bookshop@enterprise.net for details.

To order please quote title, author and ISBN
and your full name and address.
Cheques and postal orders should be made payable to 'Bookpost plc.'
Postage and packing is FREE within the UK
(overseas customers should add £1.00 per book).

Prices and availability are subject to change.